R0201834579

01/2021

D1068431

PALM BEACH COUNTY
LIBRARY SYSTEM
3650 Summit Boulevard
West Palm Beach, FL 33406-4198

SPITEFUL BONES

SPITEFUL BONES

Jeri Westerson

This first world edition published 2020
in Great Britain and 2021 in the USA by
SEVERN HOUSE PUBLISHERS LTD of
Eardley House, 4 Uxbridge Street, London W8 7SY.
Trade paperback edition first published
in Great Britain and the USA 2021 by
SEVERN HOUSE PUBLISHERS LTD.

British Library Cataloguing in Publication Data
A CIP catalogue record for this title is available from the British Library.

ISBN-13: 978-0-7278-8999-7 (cased)
ISBN-13: 978-1-78029-737-8 (trade paper)
ISBN-13: 978-1-4483-0459-2 (e-book)

All Severn House titles are printed on acid-free paper.

Severn House Publishers support the Forest Stewardship Council™ [FSC™],
the leading international forest certification organisation.
All our titles that are printed on FSC certified paper carry the FSC logo.

MIX
Paper from
responsible sources
FSC® C013056

Typeset by Palimpsest Book Production Ltd.,
Falkirk, Stirlingshire, Scotland.
Printed and bound in Great Britain by
TJ Books Limited, Padstow, Cornwall.

Author's Note

This book contains many spoilers for *Veil of Lies*, so if you haven't read it, you might wish to return to that first book in the series for a refresher before continuing with this one.

Also, it must be noted that John Rykener was a real person from Crispin's London. We first met him in *The Demon's Parchment*. We only have one document from the law rolls about him from 1395. He had been arrested, not necessarily for prostitution, but for *dressing* as a woman. In the document, he was also accused of theft and: *[He] further said that certain Phillip, rector of Theydon Garnon, had sex with him as with a woman in Elizabeth Bronderer's house outside Bishopsgate, at which time Rykener took away two gowns of Phillip, and when Phillip requested them from Rykener he said that [he] was the wife of a certain man and that if Phillip wished to ask for them back [he] would make [his] husband bring suit against him.*

We never knew the name of the husband. I have supplied it here.

Notes About Characters

Several lords in Crispin's time will be mentioned, and sometimes they were known by several different titles. For clarification, I thought it best to define them here.

Hereford – Henry Bolingbroke. Henry was the eldest son and heir to John of Gaunt, the Duke of Lancaster. He is called 'Bolingbroke' for where he was born, but he was called by several titles during his young life. In 1377 to 1397 he was styled the Earl of Derby or just 'Derby' as in earlier Crispin books. He was also the Earl of Northampton and at the same time was made Earl and Duke of Hereford, and also, briefly, the Duke of Lancaster upon his father's death. And then finally Henry IV, King of England.

Norfolk – refers to Thomas Mowbray, the Duke of Norfolk, who was earlier styled 'Nottingham'.

Gloucester – Thomas of Woodstock, brother to John of Gaunt and uncle to King Richard, was the Duke of Gloucester.

Lords Appellant – These lords (who were not called the 'Lords Appellant' in that time period) were some of Richard's great lords of England, and one was even his uncle and one his first cousin. Beginning in 1387, these lords banded together to arrest Richard's favorites who had too much sway over him and his decisions, and to control Richard's spending policies and what they saw as tyrannical tendencies. They were: Thomas of Woodstock, the Duke of Gloucester, brother of John of Gaunt (who were both sons of King Edward III), and thus Richard's uncle; Richard FitzAlan, Earl of Arundle and of Surrey; Thomas de Beauchamp, Earl of Warwick; Henry Bolingbroke, Earl of Derby (at the time), and future king of England; and Thomas Mowbray, Earl of Nottingham (at the time). After battles with these lords and after Richard was cornered in the Tower (see the Crispin books *Shadow of the Alchemist* and *The Silence of Stones*), he acquiesced to their wishes. But he never forgave their execution of his favorites, nor the injury to his ego for ordering around an anointed king.

Robert de Vere and the Battle of Radcot Bridge – Richard saw the writing on the wall in 1387 and he sent for one of his favorites, Robert de Vere, Duke of Ireland, to come to his aide when Henry and his Lords Appellant were pressing their advantage. But Henry headed him off and fought de Vere's troops at Radcot Bridge, where de Vere's army was routed and de Vere escaped into exile. Richard was furious with this outcome, because it meant that there was no stopping the Lords Appellant from forcing him to do their will.

Glossary

Cooking Powders – These are ground spices that every wealthier kitchen would have had on hand. 'White Powder' is ginger or mace blended with confectioner's sugar. 'Powder Fort' is ginger or a blend of cinnamon and mace. 'Powder Douce' is one or more of the 'sweet' spices; anise, fennel, and nutmeg. Any of these spices would often be used with meat dishes and sauces.

Divine Office or Liturgy of the Hours – In the Middle Ages, the hours were set by certain prayers offered at certain times of the day. The lay-people outside of monasteries and churches could tell what time it was by the bells calling the religious to prayer. They are (with approximate times):

Matins – Midnight to dawn
Lauds – 3 a.m.
Prime – 6 a.m.
Terce – 9 a.m.
Sext – 11 a.m./noon
None – 3 p.m.
Vespers – twilight/sundown
Compline – night/9 p.m.

Lychgate – A covered gate leading to a churchyard. *Lych* from an Old English word meaning corpse; a place a corpse would be left – sometimes for days – to await burial.

Varlet – older term for personal valet

Wattle – twigs and young branches woven together with stakes to create fences and walls that might be plastered to make smooth, solid structures.

ONE

Nigellus Cobmartin stood in the courtyard of his family home – its garden walls crumbling, its arched windows overlooking the tired and weedy garden with its dead flowers and gnarled trees – and sighed. His brother had done poorly in business and had not kept up repairs, and when *he* died only a fortnight ago, it had finally come to Nigellus. Now he wondered if it was worth salvaging.

He counted in his head the funds needed to bring the manor into a livable condition, and despaired that his law practice was still in its infancy, even though his student days were some seven years behind him.

The shadow of a woman approached and slipped her hand in his. The perfumed scent reached his nose and filled his mind and heart with pleasant thoughts and sent his worries away. She was a slender figure in a gown of simple woolens that rustled and swayed with each step of slippered feet, but a gown embroidered so elaborately that it could have easily been mistaken for a lady of highborn stature.

Except that it wasn't a woman at all, but Nigellus's lover, John Rykener. John was lean in his woman's gowns, and his skin was smooth and pale like any well-bred maiden's. Even the fullness of his lips and the arch of his brow gave him a softer appearance that fooled most men.

It had not fooled Nigellus.

'Don't worry,' John whispered in his ear. 'It will be made whole again, as it should have been all these years.'

'How lucky I am to have you by my side . . . sweet Eleanor.'

'Eleanor' was the name John insisted on using when in public. And because workmen fairly swarmed over the place, it was as public as it got.

'How your brother let it go to shit as he had . . .'

'Now, now.' He patted John's hand and glanced up at him. 'Augustus hadn't a head for money. I daresay, none of us had. Only father. And only at times. But with Augustus now gone . . .'

'I'm sorry. I didn't mean to cause you sadness. You never spoke much of your brother.'

'Never had much to say. He thought my becoming a lawyer was foolish. As foolish as if I'd joined a monastery, I suppose.'

'I'm grateful you didn't do the latter,' said John, nudging him with his elbow. His woman's gown of blues was a cote-hardie with dainty cloth buttons John had embroidered himself. 'Though I might have met you there nonetheless. My clientele practically bulged with clergy.'

'John!' he hissed. Shaking his head, he knew he seemed to admonish the daring Rykener more often than not, but he caught the edge of John's smile and knew he hadn't offended.

'Madam Cobmartin?'

John turned as a workman doffed his hat to him. It still made Nigellus uneasy to style themselves as husband and wife, but John delighted in it. 'Yes?' he said sweetly.

'We have found the plumbing and we've got men assessing the situation.'

'Oh, Nigellus! Do you hear that? Plumbing! Water running through pipes *into* the house!'

'Yes, we always had running water in the house when we were children. Be sure your men check the cistern on the roof,' he said to the workman. 'I don't have a hope that it hasn't rotted out.'

'Aye, sir. It's going to take work to get to all them lead pipes. But I say, sir, what's good enough for them Romans is good enough for Londoners.'

'Well said,' gushed Rykener.

The workman bowed, replaced his hat, and trudged back out through the courtyard arch.

John grabbed his arm and jumped up and down. 'Our very own home. With *plumbing*!'

'Anything for you, my love.'

'Oh, you are a sweet man, aren't you? How I love you.' He leaned over and gave Nigellus a loud, smacking kiss.

Nigellus felt his cheeks redden. Not that he was embarrassed to be kissed where others could see. But he was so flushed with happiness. And to think, only a brief few years before, he never imagined himself settled as they were beginning to be. He had Crispin Guest to thank for that. He never would have met the effusive Rykener if it hadn't been for London's Tracker.

They walked together arm in arm, looking over the foundations and peering up to the towers. 'What a shame that Augustus never married,' said Rykener. 'Such a big house with only him. And it truly is a fine house.'

'It *was*,' Nigellus agreed. 'I fear I shall never be able to afford to repair all of it.'

'Well, at the very least, we can make certain it's livable again.'

'That is my goal. The master carpenter said we can likely move in by as little as a fortnight.'

'I've never lived in so grand a house. Do you think it will be all right?'

Glancing at the man, Nigellus could see, despite all his spirited effusiveness, that he was nervous. He had come from a different life. A life of brothels and seamy streets, pandering to the most outrageous of clientele. John still kept the company of the infamous Elizabeth Bronderer. He had said he owed her much, teaching him the craft of embroidering . . . as well as pandering. She'd taught him to cater to women as well as men. Nigellus sometimes dreamed of bringing charges against her and putting her out of business, for he could see no good coming from it, and the priests of London would have been pleased to put down her business as well as the other stews in Southwark . . . but there were just as many other bishops and priests that were her patrons – and the Bishop of London himself owned stews – that in the end it was hardly worth the trouble.

He patted John's hand at the crook of his elbow. John may not have been raised in a household with servants attending him, but if Nigellus had anything to say about it, he'd make certain he would now. 'Of course. We already have servants,' said Nigellus, 'but, er . . . I wondered what to do about ladies' maids . . .'

'I've got it all sorted. I've already hired a woman from Madam Bronderer's house. She's around here somewhere.'

That woman again! But he smoothed his expression. 'That *is* good news.' And then he considered. 'She won't be . . . er, plying her trade here, will she?'

John stopped and gave him the look he had become familiar with. 'Under our roof? I wouldn't hear of it. She'll be making more coin as a lady's maid than as a whore at any rate, so I shouldn't think so.'

Nigellus blinked, took a deep breath, and released it. Yes, things were different with Rykener in his life. But with a shake of his head and a small smile, he decided he wouldn't have it any other way.

'Oh, there she is!' John waved at a stout, young woman with dark hair and pink cheeks. She waved back. 'Come, Susannah. Meet the master of the house.'

Susannah moved forward sluggishly and offered up a complacent smile. 'Master Nigellus,' she said.

'You must call him "Master Cobmartin", Susannah. I've told you that.'

'Aye, I forgot. What do you need, madam?'

'Nothing. I hope you're settling in.'

'I don't much like the other maid. She talks too much.'

'Well, we can't help that. But is that what you plan to wear? You mustn't look slovenly. This is a great house.'

'It's what I got, John.'

'And don't call me "John".' He looked around but there were no workmen within earshot. 'It's Madam Cobmartin.'

'I forgot.'

'Well, stop forgetting or I'll find someone else. Here.' John handed her a few coins from his own money pouch. 'Get yourself some better clothes. By the saints, I know Madam Bronderer has enough money to clothe you properly. Why hasn't she?'

Susannah shrugged. 'I'll just nip out and be back.'

'See that you do! Nigellus is terrible at helping me dress.'

She looked over Nigellus insolently, and rumbled away.

'I don't like her manner,' he whispered harshly to John.

'She's all right. She's just a bit of a grumbler.'

John took his arm again in appeasement – and it *did* appease

– as they passed under an arch that took them into the side door, where they ended up in the foyer. Nigellus raised his eyes to the tall, vaulted ceiling and the grand staircase. His father had been wealthy as a mercer, but lost nearly all his fortune later in life on dubious purchases and, of course, gambling.

'Didn't you tell me that there was supposed to be a family relic? You'd make our friend Crispin proud.'

Nigellus chuckled. 'I daresay. But it was lost some twenty years ago. Everyone believed one of our servants made off with it.'

'The churl! Whatever happened to him?'

'No idea. He ran off. I was but a lad of fifteen at the time. Oh, it was the scandal. How father raved. I was set to learn my father's trade, but I had begged instead to learn the law. Father didn't see the sense in it, but he handed over the coin anyway. I'll always be grateful for that. He wanted me to be happy, bless him. And in any case, Augustus was the older son. He was set to inherit the mercer business. So it little mattered what I got up to.'

'I'm glad you became a lawyer . . . and a fine one you are! I can't see you as a merchant. Though you are getting a bit round in the middle.' He poked Nigellus in the gut. He sputtered.

'John, behave yourself.'

'I thought you liked it when I *mis*behaved,' he said quietly, waggling his brows.

Nigellus blushed again and John giggled at it.

'Have you done with the embroidery of the bed covers?' said Nigellus conversationally, hoping to change the subject.

'Nearly. It's a big job. I had to hire help. But they were my friends and happy to do it. I daresay they're happy for me. Seldom do whores make out as well as I have.'

He didn't like to think of that aspect of John's life. He'd been a whore longer than he'd known Nigellus, and besides the occasional work as an embroideress, John filled his time with the paid company of men . . . and women. Nigellus hoped that once they were settled down, he'd quit this other business and be a proper . . . well, wife, for all intents and purposes.

'So what was this relic anyway?' asked John. 'Was it

something gruesome? I can't say I approve of severed heads and limbs.' He shivered. 'I know that the Church seems to love these things, but those belong in a church, not one's home.'

'It was nothing like that. My father made one pilgrimage to Rome and there he obtained the hair of Saint Elmo . . . for his colic. I'm afraid it didn't seem to do him much good. But the reliquary was a lovely crystal sheath, about so big—' He fashioned the size with his hands, the size of one of his palms. 'With gold and gems atop and below. We reckoned the servant made off with it to sell for its precious reliquary.'

'Hair. That's not so bad. I once saw the relic of a saint's *face*. It was ghastly. I completely forgot to pray once laying eyes upon it. But I was young at the time.'

'And so very grown-up now.'

'You tease me. But I tell you, this will be a grand manor. I will work hard to make it so.'

'Don't spend your money,' he said quietly. 'You keep it. My practice is doing very well these days.'

'And you are such a dear. Don't think I don't know what's behind it. You'd like me to retire.'

He ducked his head, unwilling for John to see him blush yet again. 'And so . . . you know me well.'

'And love you best. But it does make me a good living.'

'And an illegal one. And me a lawyer. It doesn't sit well.'

John fell silent. This argument was familiar territory. Nigellus supposed they needn't tread it again.

Someone called out upstairs. It didn't sound much like a workman simply calling to another. It had the sound of true alarm about it. Both he and John rushed to the bottom of the stairs and looked up.

A workman came running to the gallery above and pointed back from where he had come. Other men rushed down the passage. Then more men came running.

'Whatever is this to-do?' said John.

But even as Nigellus was set to answer him, another workman hurled himself down the stairs and skidded to a halt in front of him. 'Please, sir. You must come.'

'What is the matter?'

'You must come, sir.'

He gave John a look and they both climbed the stairs together, following the anxious workman, who kept looking back to make certain they were close behind. Nigellus led the way. It was the north wing – the last one his father had built all those years ago. Peeking here and there at the work that had been done in the last few days, he was glad that it was only being repaired and not built from the ground up. As good as his practice was, it never would have been good enough to build from the beginning. No, his family home only made him *look* grand, for he wasn't as wealthy as his father had been. Nothing of the kind.

They entered into another passage and Nigellus could see that the wall had been demolished . . . or it had crumbled away. There was rubble of plaster and broken wattle on the floor and men stood around the gaping hole, crossing themselves and murmuring softly.

'What is this, gentlemen?' asked Nigellus in as officious a tone as he could muster.

When the men parted, he could see the hole in the wall. A gaping hole, as big as a doorway, in fact. But there was something there amid the shadows. As he drew closer and the men stepped aside, he gasped.

Folded within was a skeleton, crouched and stuffed within the posts. The skull grinned salaciously, as if its secrets were being spilled out at last for all to hear. And yet, the lay of the bones spoke another tale. For there were the barest remnants of what looked to be ropes tied around the bones of the wrists as well as the feet. And in the bound hands was the glint of gold. Nigellus stepped up and stood before it.

The gold and precious gems of the reliquary, missing from his father's estate nearly twenty years ago. Along with, evidently, the servant who had stolen it.

Nigellus could only stare. Surely he was not seeing this. This couldn't be true.

Beside him, John sputtered. 'What . . . what . . .'

He took John's hand and squeezed it. 'Eleanor,' he said softly. 'You'd best fetch the sheriff.'

'To hell with that,' John breathed. 'I'm getting Crispin Guest!'

TWO

Crispin Guest bounced little Gilbert Tucker on his knee. The three-year-old giggled and laughed outright as Crispin made horse sounds. 'Hold tight to the reins, Gilbert,' he said, squeezing the boy's hands. The child squeezed back. 'The enemy is just ahead. Lean down with your lance. Lean!' The boy was laughing so much that he slid off Crispin's leg entirely and rolled on the floor, still laughing.

Crispin peered over his thighs and cocked his head at the child. 'That's no way to sit a horse. You've lost the joust.'

Isabel Tucker's shadow suddenly fell over him and he looked up. Her brown hair was neatly arranged under a spotless kerchief, and her green woolen gown – though nothing like new – was in good order. Fine tears had been skillfully mended and if patches there were, none were detectable. As always, her belly was slightly plump with another of Jack's babes. Despite this, Madam Tucker was always presentable, a feat Crispin appreciated all the more with a cadre of children around her who, regardless of what they ate, seemed constantly to have sticky hands and faces.

She had a wooden spoon in one hand, and baby Genevieve tucked in the other arm. 'Master Guest, I shall do everything in my power to make certain that boy does *not* go to war. On a horse or otherwise.'

Crispin sat back, affronted. 'Madam, I have fought many a time and it didn't do me any harm.'

Her expression when she turned said it all. The tilt of her brow, the set of her lips. He felt properly chastised. He eyed that wooden spoon warily. No wonder Jack did as he was told. He was far more obedient under his wife's gaze than he ever was under Crispin's scrutiny.

It was just as well. His back ached from playing with the child, who suddenly seemed preoccupied with a wooden toy horse. Crispin rose and stretched. One of his wrists ached as well. It seemed to ache most days and twinged when he tried to use it. It was the one he'd broken some fifteen years ago. Well, at forty-three, what did he expect? He was getting old, no mistaking it. He noticed there was more gray in his black hair these days, mostly at his temples. The hair hadn't thinned – God be praised! It was as luxurious as it had been when he was a much younger man. Jack had told him the gray made him look distinguished. He had clouted him for that observation.

'Isabel, was Christopher coming today or was it tomorrow?'

'Today, you said, sir. It's about the time he'll be here. Shall I serve the good wine?'

'No, the lad should have ale. I'd not return him to his mother in his cups.'

'He's a fine lad, Master Crispin. He'll not pick up any bad habits around you, sir.'

Not anymore, he thought with some pride. He'd stopped indulging in his misery of getting drunk in Isabel's uncle's tavern, the Boar's Tusk, years ago. He had a family to provide for now. And anyway, it had been years since he had felt sorry for himself. His life had much improved from the time he had been banished from court. That had been some twenty years ago. A whole lifetime. Half *his* life, at any rate. What did he have to complain about these days except for a few aches and pains?

He went to the back garden and to the shed where the horses sometimes spent their nights. But Seb, Jack's horse, and Tobias, Crispin's, as usual grazed in their garden. The children were wont to bedevil them, but the beasts were gentle and didn't seem to mind.

Crispin kept his wooden practice swords in the shed. The swords were something he had acquired in exchange for some work to a swordmaker. He delighted in teaching his son the art of a knight, even if he couldn't acknowledge the boy. He could at least offer him the gift of his skills, such as they were. Jack benefitted as well, for he could learn properly the swordsmanship Crispin had tried to impart to him over the years, using sticks instead of proper practice swords. Not that Jack would ever be able to afford a sword of his own. Ah, well. Once Crispin was gone, Jack would inherit *his* sword.

It was the least he could do for the lad who had given him so much over the years.

'Is Christopher on his way?' said Jack, coming through the garden gate. He reached over to Seb and patted the horse's flank. The man was lank and tall, taller than Crispin, with a shock of ginger hair in curls flopping over his freckled forehead. He sported a carefully clipped beard and looked every bit the formidable guardian Crispin certainly would have had around him when he was a lord. Crispin counted himself fortunate that Jack had come into his life all those years ago.

'He should be here shortly.'

'He's growing to a fine lad.'

'Yes, he is.' And even though he called another man 'father', Crispin was proud of the boy that was his own blood.

Christopher had become part of the fabric of Crispin's life on the Shambles. He hadn't believed it could be possible, but after all, the boy insisted on visiting Crispin, the man he knew was his real father. Jack welcomed him into his family as if he were his own. Crispin chuckled a little at the thought. For Jack had seemed to do the same to Crispin. Wasn't it Crispin who had taken Jack in as a servant all those years ago? But then Jack married Isabel and brought her into their household. Then children came and Crispin was no longer their master, but the patriarch. He couldn't have been more amused. If someone had told him that he would be beholden to his own servant back when he was a wealthy lord, he certainly would have laughed at the notion.

'Will you stay to help?'

'Aye, sir. If that is your will.'

'I do not mean to take you from your other duties.'

'Oh. Right. I'd best ask Isabel first.'

Isabel ran his household with an iron hand, and she was not above taking Crispin to task for interrupting it. How times had changed him. He never would have allowed them these liberties. And never would he have known Jack's wife or his children being mere servants in his hall.

Now he couldn't imagine life without them.

Jack returned, looking much relieved. 'It seems I do have the time, master.' He brought the jug of ale and several cups.

'How kind of her to give you permission.'

Jack pulled up short and raised a flushed face. 'Oh. Master Crispin, I . . .'

But Crispin burst out laughing. 'She's got us both cowed, Tucker. We've got rings in our noses and there's nothing for it.'

'But sir, she shouldn't do that to you. I've told her hundreds of times . . .'

'It doesn't matter. You know it doesn't. She's only gotten it from you.'

'Now that's not true—'

'You see? You naysay me. Should a servant ever naysay his master with the frequency you do so to me? I am cowed by all my servants.'

Jack shook his head and set the jug down, pouring two cups. 'You've only yourself to blame, sir. You tried beating it out of me, but I am stubborn, God knows.'

'That you are, Tucker.'

Jack smiled and handed Crispin the first cup. 'To your health, sir. God keep you.'

'And you,' said Crispin, saluting with his cup, and then drank.

'What's this?' asked the dark-haired lad passing through the back door. 'Drinking in the middle of the afternoon, Master Jack? And you, Master Crispin, encouraging him.'

Crispin poured ale into the third cup and handed it to his son. 'And don't forget yours.'

He took it, glanced once over his shoulder, surely looking out for his mother, and drank a dose. He set it aside and rubbed his hands together. 'I've been looking forward to this all morning.'

'And so you should,' said Crispin, fetching the wooden swords. 'You excel at it.'

'I have a good teacher.' He winked.

Each day the boy grew to look more and more like Crispin. The same black hair, the same slate gray eyes, the same sharp nose, even the same swagger and other mannerisms. It both flattered and frightened him. He did not wish for the boy's place to be taken from him as Crispin's had been stripped away. At fourteen, the boy was the beneficiary of the life of a wealthy merchant. It could so easily be despoiled if his father, Clarence Walcote, got wind of his true paternity.

He wiped away all dark thoughts. For the boy was with him for now. His son. Sharp in wit as Crispin was, and nimble with a sword. He would give the boy all he had . . . save his name.

'Flattery,' said Crispin, 'will not make me go any easier on you.' He took up one of the wooden swords and twirled it expertly over his wrist.

Christopher watched with open mouth.

Jack leaned into the boy. 'He's showing off. Just do like I showed you before.'

Christopher took the wooden sword from Jack . . . and heaved it toward Crispin, point first.

Crispin stumbled forward and righted his blade in time to smack the other out of the way. 'It's not fair, Tucker, to teach him your dirty tricks.'

'Dirty tricks *you* taught *me*, sir,' said Jack, laughing.

Crispin tossed the blade back to Christopher. 'Jack is correct, of course. It is all well to act the gentleman with all courtesy when in the public eye, but when engaged in a fight, remember it is for your life. You need not be polite or politic. If a man loses his blade or falls to the ground, make certain he stays there at all costs. I've shown you before how to handle the blade in all situations; how to use it like a club or a crook when the opportunity presents itself. Don't forget any of those tactics, boy. Now. Ready yourself.'

Christopher postured, sword up at eye level with bent elbow, point facing Crispin, his left hand steadying the hilt.

Crispin nodded at his form and crouched into his position, ready to attack . . . when a commotion in the house caught his attention. And that's when Christopher struck.

The wooden blade came at him, and Crispin's instinct kicked in. He batted the blade away with a downward stroke, and came back with an upswinging strike, caught Christopher's blade, and pulled it from his hand, tossing it away.

'How did you—'

But Isabel rushed to the back door, soon followed by another, taller woman, who burst past her and stumbled in front of Crispin, muddy skirts swaying.

'Crispin!' cried the woman.

Crispin elbowed Jack and his apprentice tried to look equally chastened, but it wasn't quite working.

Nigellus trotted up the stairs and joined them. He was a slight young man with a serious comportment and the somewhat threadbare attire of the long black gown and black cap of a lawyer. His eyes, as always, were bright with a mind that delighted in learning, even if it seemed at times somewhat scattered. Still, Crispin was glad to call him friend, even though he and the eccentric Rykener lived together as they did.

'Master Crispin, I am sore glad to see you, sir.' He gestured toward the bones. 'What's to be done? What, by the mass, happened here?'

Crispin leaned in and touched what looked like the remnants of a cloth gag trailing from the mandible. 'Well, I think you know as well as I, Master Cobmartin, that this was murder.'

'In my father's house. In the very walls! By all the saints, the man died here, even as we all went about living *our* lives. It's . . . it's . . .'

'Horrible,' gasped John, taking his arm.

Crispin scrutinized the interior of the wall, and the plaster that was torn away. 'This must have made a stink.'

'There was always something with this house,' said Nigellus. 'The roof leaked, the cistern leaked – and a horrendous smell *that* made! There were rats. I don't recall any time of any particular strong odor, but there were always rats dying within the walls. Once we found a cat.'

'But John said this was your father's room.'

'He wasn't here all that often. During the construction, he wasn't here at all. Left it to the architect to take care of all of it. In fact, he had been traveling for months around that time. I was just beginning at Gray's Inn, so I wasn't here either.'

'You wouldn't recall his name, would you? The man in the wall?'

Nigellus nodded. 'Wilfrid, his name was. Wilfrid Roke. He was such a loyal man. No one could believe it, but he was gone and so was the relic, *ipso facto*. My father was heartbroken.'

Crispin swept his gaze over the wall, the skeleton, the ceiling and open rafters. 'You say this servant disappeared some twenty years ago?'

'Yes, I remember it well. It was quite the household scandal at the time. The relic was stolen – and my father ranted and raved about that as he had undertaken a long and costly journey to obtain it, and he a very congenial man – and then Wilfrid disappeared. We all assumed it was he who stole it and ran off. Oh, my father was saddened and disappointed. Father left for business travel directly after the incident. Wilfrid was my father's varlet, you see, and very trusted. I'm afraid it made it very hard on Wilfrid's son, who remained in service to the household. He is here still.'

'This man's son still works here?'

'Yes. Shall I fetch him?'

'Do that. But, er, have a regard for the circumstances.'

Nigellus seemed to put on the mask of a barrister and comported his face into the proper attitude before walking off.

Crispin tapped Jack and pulled him aside. 'Keep a good eye on the son to see how he reacts.'

'Blind me, sir. He's about to see his own sire's bones. I expect him to react rather badly.'

'Just so. But see what else you can observe.'

'What are you whispering about?' said Christopher, poking his head in.

'Tracker talk,' said Crispin.

'I want to know, too. I'm going to be a Tracker someday.'

'Christopher, I've told you before. You are a merchant's son. Be a merchant. A Tracker lives the life of a poor man.'

'You don't look poor to me. You're not in rags. You and Jack have a healthy family and you're all happy.'

Crispin turned helplessly to Jack, and Jack took the hint. He touched Christopher on the shoulders and steered him away. 'Now, Master Walcote, you know better. Master Crispin has told you time and again. Maybe I should take you home . . .'

'No, Jack! I'll stay. I'll be quiet. I promise.'

'See that you do, lad.' He winked at Crispin, but Crispin wasn't mollified.

Nigellus arrived back at the stair's landing with a young man, about Jack's age. His brown eyes darted here and there, and he twisted the hem of his tunic in his ink-stained hands.

'This is William Roke,' said Nigellus. 'He has served the household as a clerk for a number of years.'

'What is this about, Master Cobmartin? I've only just come from the marketplace and all the workmen here are making a to-do.'

'This is Crispin Guest, William. You may have heard me mention him. He's the Tracker of London.'

William bowed, still looking perplexed.

Crispin and Jack stood in front of the hole in the wall, blocking the remains from view. 'William,' Crispin began, 'what do you recall of your father's disappearance?'

'My *father*? Master Guest, that was years and years ago. I was five years old at the time. I scarce remember him at all.'

'Do you remember the circumstances of his disappearance? What he might have said? Who he talked to?'

William glanced toward Nigellus again. 'Master Cobmartin, what is this about? I barely remember my father, let alone the circumstances when he left.' He turned back to Crispin. 'My mother died and then my father disappeared. It was a terrible time. I could have been left on my own, no one to see to me, but Master Cobmartin's father kindly took me in and the servants raised me. Master Cobmartin here taught me my letters, gave me a vocation.'

Much as Crispin had done for Jack. He felt his apprentice at his side, though he didn't turn toward him. Instead, he flicked a glance at Nigellus who lowered his eyes and flushed with embarrassment.

'And a noble thing it was of your masters to do, both father and son. But William, if you cannot offer any insight as to your father's disappearance, is there anyone in this household who can?'

He wrinkled his brow. 'I don't know why you are asking this. It was too long ago.'

'Because . . . because your father has been found.'

'What? Is he here? Where is he?'

'I'm very much afraid, Master Roke, that your father . . . is dead.' He stepped aside, revealing the bones.

William threw his hand over his mouth. 'No! Holy Mother Mary! Is that . . . is that . . . *him*?'

'Steady, William,' said Nigellus, placing his hands on the man's shoulders. 'The workmen found him. I am heartily sorry for this. May God have mercy on him.'

'Oh, blessed saints,' the man murmured. He walked forward, peering at the bones in their repose. 'Wait . . . is he . . . *tied* up? Master Tracker,' he said, tearing his eyes away for a mere moment to look at Crispin, before staring at the bones once more. 'What does this mean?'

'It means your father was murdered twenty years ago. And if I can, I will try to discover who could have done it.'

'And I will pay your fee, Master Guest,' said Nigellus.

'My father was murdered,' said William, fingers touching his lips. He shook his head. He stared at the bones as if trying to discern the man they used to be. 'I scarce remember him. Is that a sin? Honor thy father and thy mother. I *have* honored him. At least I tried. I've prayed for him. But since he was a thief and dishonored himself, I tried mostly to forget him. And now . . . if he wasn't a thief all those years ago, I have done him a grave injustice.' He looked to Nigellus. 'Does that make me a sinful man?'

'I am no cleric,' said Nigellus, placing a gentle hand on the young man's shoulder once more, 'but I can't think it is a sin not to remember your parents when you last saw them as a little child. And we all thought him a . . . well. As you said, we thought he had stolen away the relic. How can our Lord fault you – or us – for that?'

He seemed somewhat relieved but still troubled. 'I was taken in by the old steward and his wife. But they died, him eight years ago and she two years, bless them.'

'There must be others,' said Nigellus. 'Scullions, chambermaids, gardeners, cooks . . .'

'Yes, Master Cobmartin. The cook. He is the same from those days, I think. Shall I get him?'

'Yes. But . . . don't bring him here. Let us go to the parlor below. And William . . . I *am* sorry.'

William ducked his head. 'I'm very glad my father was not a thief. That does my heart very well indeed. After all these years . . .'

Crispin said nothing. For he didn't wish to break this man's heart a second time. Simply because his father was murdered did not mean he *hadn't* stolen the relic.

He suddenly looked up at Crispin. 'Master Guest, you are the celebrated Tracker. Find that murderer as quick as you can, sir.'

'Master Roke, I will do my best.'

He bowed to Crispin and then John Rykener before he trotted down the stairs.

'*Abiit nemine salutato*,' said Nigellus, ticking his head again at the remains in the wall.

'He couldn't very well bid no one farewell when he was murdered,' offered Jack.

'True, Master Jack. Well, Crispin. You have your work cut out for you on this one.'

'Fee or no, Master Cobmartin – though I thank you for that.' He bowed. 'Contrary to what I just told the son, I don't know whether after all this time I will be able to solve this mystery. All the clues are long gone. The murderer might even be dead. And . . . I haven't ruled out that your father's varlet *wasn't* a thief.'

'Dear me,' said Nigellus, worry lines stepping up his forehead again.

'The clues aren't *all* gone,' said Jack, approaching the skeleton again and scrutinizing closely. '*He's* the clue, right here.'

'Indeed. Perhaps the only clue we'll have. What do you observe, Jack?'

'Well . . . he was bound at his wrists and his ankles.' He touched the wispy remains of the cloth in the teeth. 'And gagged. Oh. Look here.' He pulled a silver cross on a leather cord from the detritus on his chest. In its center was a small black jewel. He held it away from the bones and showed it to Crispin.

'His son should have that,' Crispin said.

'Shall I take it now, sir? You know how them sheriff's men can be.'

Crispin did know. How often had he noted that a corpse's belongings somehow disappeared after the sheriff's serjeants got a hold of the body for the coroner.

'Best do so.'

Carefully, Jack extricated it from the desiccated clothes where it had clearly lain on the man's chest. He clutched the necklace for but a moment and stuffed it into his pouch.

'And the relic,' said Crispin.

Jack turned once more to the bones. In the spindly fingers the reliquary lay unmolested but dusty and stained from the decaying remains. Jack hesitated before reaching for the crystal vial. With delicate fingers – fingers that for years had stolen many a purse or the contents within, Crispin noted – Jack grasped the crystal cylinder and gently pulled. The hands didn't seem to want to give it up, and for a moment, Jack seemed struck with puzzlement as to what to do. Thankfully, the dead hands gave up their prize at last and fell away, releasing the crystal and its long chain.

Jack peered at it close to his nose before he handed it to Crispin. Now it was his turn to examine it. Cloudy crystal harbored a lock of curled hair, brown. Supposedly from Saint Elmo. The top of the crystal was fashioned with a gold cap, encrusted with gemstones, and at the other end was the same. He turned it in his hands – a thing weighing so little on its own – and turned to Nigellus. 'Your family relic, Master Cobmartin.'

'Oh. Yes. God be p-praised.' Nigellus took it in both hands, though he looked reluctant to touch it. And now that he had it, he didn't seem to know what to do with it. He showed it to John, but his companion took a step back, unwilling to touch it. Nigellus finally, and with as much reverence as he could muster, placed it in the pouch secured to his belt. He wore a grimace, no doubt from touching the thing that bore witness to a death . . . and the decay of the man he had once known.

Jack continued his examination of the skull and ran a finger along the top of the cranium. Though Jack gave pause at a newly made corpse, bones did not seem to trouble him as they once had. 'Ah, look here. A bit of a crack. Could have happened after he died in the decomposing. But it looks as if someone coshed him good. Aye, look at the wood of the uprights here. If he was still awake, there would be scratches and scuffs from a struggle. There's naught.'

'Very good, Jack.' Crispin looked where Jack pointed at the wooden frame. There *should* have been scratches, dents from kicking at least. He could have been knocked unconscious to stuff him within, and without ever wakening, he simply died. Being shut up in such close circumstances – woven wattle and plaster – it would have been hot and suffocating surrounds. Even if he had awakened, he might easily have smothered. 'And if all that were so,' he said, gently touching the bones, 'then whoever did this was likely part of the company of workmen and knew how to plaster a wall.'

'Aye. There is that.'

'And more than that,' Crispin went on. 'You see here. There is no wattle. Either it was meant as a door or an alcove, or the murderer made certain there was room within the wall for the body. Looks like straw and plaster. I'm certain the lime in the plaster made short work of the flesh. Or the rats did.'

Christopher poked his head into the opening of the wall, nudging Crispin aside. 'That's horrible,' he said, with still no trace of horror in his eyes. 'Then the killer worked here. How diabolical. He patched this wall without ever saying a word. And secretly, he knew that time would kill the man within. But why didn't he take the relic, then?'

Crispin was about to admonish the boy to keep silent when he thought about his words. 'Yes. Why not take the relic?' Jewels encrusted the gold caps above and below the crystal cylinder. 'The reliquary alone would be worth a small fortune. And everyone would assume this man took it.'

Christopher looked up at Crispin with a widening grin. 'This is what you do all the time, isn't it? Look at corpses and puzzle out who did it. This is far more interesting than being a mercer.'

'But it pays far less. Come, Christopher. You promised to be quiet. Especially now that we must interrogate the cook.'

'I'll be quiet. I want to watch and learn.'

God save me, Crispin thought.

They trudged down the steps and met not just workmen, but part of the household: a maid, gardener, stablemen, all trying to catch a glimpse of what might be upstairs. Nigellus shooed them away and they scattered, trotting in different directions. Crispin watched them go and shook his head. It was a gruesome discovery, but it was by far one of the more interesting things to have happened to the household. He couldn't blame them for wanting to see it first-hand.

They came to the parlor, where they awaited the cook. It was a modest and pleasant room on the ground floor with tall windows painting a slant of sunlight upon the tiled floor. Crispin couldn't help but recall that he had had a room similar to this as his own study, a place for his few books and to go over the household accounts with his steward. The room smelled of the low fire in the hearth and the comfort of spiced wine and the subtle perfumes of the men who came to do business at the Cobmartin household.

When he glanced toward his son, he noted that Christopher, though throbbing with energy, kept his promise to keep silent. Hopping a bit on the balls of his feet, he scanned Crispin, Jack, Nigellus and even Rykener. And all the while, his eyes seemed to gleam with an inner intelligence, perhaps trying to work it all out for himself.

Presently, a mild-mannered man entered the parlor, his hands on his apron, looking about curiously. His nose was large like a beak and his eyes were sunk into dark sockets framed by bushy gray brows. 'Master Cobmartin, madam . . .' He bowed to Rykener. 'You called me forth?'

'Yes,' said Nigellus, puffing himself up like a lawyer at the bar. He even grasped the lapel of his gown and stared down his nose at the man. Crispin tried to catch his eye but he was too focused on the cook. 'Master Robert.'

'Aye, sir. God bless you, sir.'

'Now, Robert, I wonder if you could cast your mind back some twenty years ago. You were a cook in my father's household, yes?'

'Twenty years ago? Aye, my lord. I was new to the kitchens in this household, but I hope I did my job well. I moved up in the ranks, so to speak. I became head cook . . . let me think . . . ten years ago. Your father, lord bless him, never had any reason to complain. The food was always hot and spiced just how he liked it. There was never a rotten haunch or a stinking bit of fish in this household. No, sir!'

'Yes, yes, quite. But . . . if you can remember – and indeed, even *I* have a difficult time – when Wilfrid Roke ran off with the relic—'

'Oh lord, yes! What a damnable time that was, begging your

mercy, madam.' He bowed again to John who gave him the generous smile of the matron of the house. 'That was a terrible time indeed. Your sire . . . oh, he was fierce mad at Wilfrid. We all were. It comes down hard on the whole house when a servant does wrong. It gives all of us a black eye, so to speak. But why . . .'

'He was found, Robert.'

Robert froze and blinked. It was then he took in the rest in the parlor, Crispin and Jack and Christopher. He grew quiet. 'What does this mean, Master Nigellus?' he said in a less blustery tone.

'We have found his *remains* in the house, Robert. He didn't run off with the relic after all. He was murdered.'

'Oh, lord!' His face was open and wide with shock. Such a thing would have been easy to create a false face, thought Crispin, but this man did not look as if he were mumming a part.

'So is it possible, Robert, that you remember something from that time, even some little thing, some bit of information that you might have thought trivial? Anything could now be of great import.'

'If I may?' said Crispin, stepping forward.

'Robert, this is Crispin Guest. He is the Tracker of London and, as you may well know, he discovers such secrets that lead to the king's justice, finding the culprits of heinous crimes.'

Robert's mouth was formed into an 'O' of surprise as he stared long and hard at Crispin.

'And so, Master Robert,' said Crispin, settling himself with feet apart, thumbs tucked into his belt. 'As your master suggests, any little thing you can recall could be of utmost importance. Perhaps some theory discussed amongst the other servants . . .'

'There was some speculation. I was five and twenty or so at the time and full of ambition. But two of the maids wondered if he hadn't run off with the third maid. She went missing too.'

Nigellus lost his mask of the barrister and leaned toward Robert. 'A maid missing? I don't recall that.'

'It was not long after poor Wilfrid's wife died. Poor Margaret Roke. Such a sad thing. Maybe the ado didn't reach your sire's ear. But no doubt the steward knew of it. I think you were gone to the lawyer's school by then, sir.'

Crispin turned to Nigellus. 'And the steward of that time?'

The man shook his head. 'Dead. Died eight years ago. We have the house records, but he wouldn't know unless there was a notation taken.'

'House records?' asked Crispin, his eyes brightening.

'House records,' muttered Nigellus. 'By the Rood! Where is Philip? Robert, fetch Philip Able. But also think hard on anything else you might have heard of during that time.'

Robert bowed to everyone, and was about to scurry off to find the steward when Crispin stopped him.

'Robert, what was the name of the missing maid?'

'Her name was Ardath.' He rushed out after that.

'Our former steward was meticulous in his records of our household,' said Nigellus excitedly. 'I was always following the poor man around, and I learned at his knee how to keep records, which came in very handy indeed when I went into the law. Ah, how I miss Justin. He died of the sweating sickness. He was a very valuable man. Very valuable.'

Rykener patted his shoulder in sympathy and Nigellus unconsciously clutched at that hand with affection.

Crispin glanced back at Christopher, wide-eyed and intrigued with each new discovery. Was it merely the novelty? Or was it something in him, in his blood, that made him so captivated, as Crispin had been, by investigating crimes? It reminded him that he had his family ring to leave behind. Would it be foolish to leave it to Christopher and risk discovery of who he really was? This he would need to discuss with Nigellus if he were to prepare a will for him.

It wasn't long till the steward entered. Philip Able was a reedy man, with long arms and long fingers, a sallow complexion, with a thin nose and equally thin lips. Crispin thought he could do with a beard to fill out his face, but the man instead sported a deep shadow of a beard instead. His gown was long and was of wool in a dark russet color. He wore the cap of a clerk. A set of keys on a ring and a pen case hung from his belt, displaying his importance in the household.

He bowed to Nigellus, and gave a polite tilt of the head to the rest of Crispin's company.

'Philip,' said Nigellus all in a rush, 'we must see the

household records from twenty years ago, when Wilfrid Roke disappeared with my father's relic. I'm certain you recall it. Can you bring them?'

His eyes scanned judiciously over Crispin, Jack, and Christopher. 'My lord, it would be simpler to bring you to my offices. The scrolls are many.'

Nigellus nodded. 'Oh, indeed. Of course. Let's do that.' As they followed Philip from the parlor, Nigellus motioned back toward Crispin. 'This is Crispin Guest, the Tracker of London, and this is his man, Jack Tucker. And, er, Christopher Walcote, a mercer.'

Philip's brow ticked at that last pronouncement but his face never changed. They followed him down a corridor and around a corner under the stairs. Philip took his key ring and deftly found the proper key, turning it with a small sound of scraping in the lock. He opened the heavy door held together with iron hinges arrayed in curls and florets and a grid of square nails peppering the wood. He allowed Nigellus and his guests in first, and they arranged themselves around a clerk's high, slanted table. Philip entered and went straight to a set of shelves piled high with scrolls, their long leather tags hanging over each shelf like locks of hair, they were so numerous. A small, murky fire in the hearth made the room dim with a veiling layer of smoke and there was only one small window for light to try to break through the dimness. A candle on the desk valiantly burned its small flame, but the smokiness was nearly too much for it.

Christopher coughed and then tried to cover it by clearing his throat.

'Now let me see,' said Philip, using a finger to scan his shelves of scrolls and leather-clad volumes. 'As I recall, Master Cobmartin, this all occurred in April of 1378, is that correct?'

'Yes, April. It took ever so long a time to get the household back into some sort of semblance of order. My father looked grayer than he ever had been before that terrible year.'

'Generally, the scrolls from one year are sewn together,' said Philip, dithering at the shelf, pulling one scroll out and looking at it before putting it back, and repeating the process. 'But Master Justin took so many notes that it became unwieldy, and so they were divided into three, or thereabouts, depending on the information.' He studied the shelf back and forth and muttered, 'Hmm. Curious.' He ran his hand over the length of scrolls on one shelf and went to the next, looking at the leather tags and tutting all the while.

'This is very curious,' he said again.

'What is it, man?' asked Nigellus. 'Can't you find the scrolls?'

'Well . . . that's just the thing.' He turned to his master apologetically. 'I . . . it's never happened before. But I cannot seem to find *any* scroll from that year. Here is 1377 and these are all from 1379. But that particular year . . . seems to be missing.'

'But that's absurd!' cried Nigellus, and he cast himself forward and rummaged through the scrolls himself, much to the quiet consternation of his steward.

As they searched, Crispin turned his attention to the hearth. The fire was unduly smoky and as he crouched and looked, he could see why. He drew his knife and teased a burning parchment scroll from the flames and dumped it upon the tiled floor. 'Look here.'

Philip's eyes enlarged and he fell upon the burning scroll. He patted out the flames but it only scattered into blackened cinders. 'But . . . what . . .'

Crispin stirred the ashes and found what remained of charred leather tags. 'Are these the scrolls you sought?'

'But . . .' The man's long fingers were blackened from soot as he sifted through the ashes on the floor. 'Why would someone burn these? They were *household* records. They should never be touched by anyone but the steward.'

'Indeed,' said Crispin, rising and sheathing his dagger. 'Your master seemed to think that these were more than mere household accountings.'

'Why yes. My predecessor kept the records more or less as also a journal of events and happenings in the house. They were most interesting and detailed. I tried to follow in his footsteps, observing and recording all that transpires, not merely the income and outlay of daily expenses. But this! What a waste. A tragic waste. Who could have done it?'

'Who indeed?' said Crispin. 'Who has a key to this door?'

'No one,' he said primly. 'Only me and Master or Madam

Cobmartin.' He held up his own key as proof, even though he had only just now opened the door under their eyes.

Crispin turned toward Nigellus with an eye toward John. 'Do either of you still have your keys?'

John looked down at the key ring at his belt, like any proper chatelaine, and Nigellus did the same to his key ring. 'All accounted for,' said Nigellus, puzzled. 'And you . . . Eleanor?'

Rykener shook his head, his veil swaying with each movement. 'They're all here.'

'These scrolls were burned just now,' said Crispin. 'And that can mean only one thing. Whoever had knowledge of this murder is still in this house.'

FOUR

'But master,' said Jack, looking from the fireplace to the door. 'That's a crime from twenty years ago. Who would still be here and worried they'd be found out after all this time?'

'Don't you know, Jack?' said Crispin. 'Why, the murderer, of course.'

'No. No, that is absurd,' said Nigellus. 'So many of those who were here twenty years ago are dead or gone from the household.'

Crispin thumbed the pommel of his dagger, rubbing it unconsciously. 'Well, it may not be the murderer himself, but someone here with knowledge, trying to protect them.' He happened to glance toward Christopher who was doing his best to conceal his smile.

When he caught Crispin's eye, he didn't bother trying to hide it anymore. 'This is very exciting,' he said, though after he'd said it, he composed his face to bland regard again.

Crispin couldn't help but wink at the lad and then straightened his face as well. 'Discovering the dead man's remains has begun a sequence of events. Someone here assumed no one would find the body, but now that we have . . . I advise caution, Nigellus.' He gestured toward the burned scrolls. 'Someone has seen to it that we find out as little as possible.'

'We'll have to question everyone in the house,' said Jack. 'Every blessed one of them.'

'Jack's right,' said Crispin.

But there was a commotion at the door and shouting. They rushed from the steward's office and headed toward the front entry.

Both sheriffs stood in the foyer, looking around. 'Where is the master of this house?' shouted Sheriff William Askham. 'Or the sarding steward?' His round voice carried to the back walls and even to the rafters, for workmen appeared over the top of the gallery and looked down. Crispin knew he was a fishmonger and likely used to calling out his wares on the bustling streets of London. He was a big man, more like a smith with his broad shoulders, solid head that seemed to miss a neck entirely and simply blend into those shoulders. The man liked his furs and velvets and long necklaces of gold worn over all.

Sheriff John Woodcock stood off to the side, a slight man with delicate features, sandy, wiry hair and dead blue eyes, with an air of indifference about him whenever he fulfilled his charge; scrolled nose in the air, lower lip protruding, eyes squinting. Perhaps, pondered Crispin, Sheriff Askham had the odor of fish about him and close proximity wore on Sheriff Woodcock.

Askham's eyes fell on Crispin and his face blotched suddenly with red. 'I might have known,' he rumbled. 'Guest! Stand before me and explain.'

Crispin straightened his crimson cote-hardie and approached both sheriffs, bowing gracefully. 'My lords, there has been a murder in this house.'

'That much we knew, Guest,' said Askham impatiently. 'Well? Where is it?'

'Up yon staircase.'

'Then I suppose we should examine the body.' He made a reluctant move toward the stairs.

'There isn't much of a body, my lords,' said Crispin, stopping him.

Sheriff Askham scowled and glanced toward his companion. 'It's Guest up to his old tricks again, I'll wager. Very well. I'll play your little game and much grief you'll get from me and my serjeants about it. Just *why* isn't there "much of a body"?'

'Because it is merely a skeleton. Stuffed into a cavity in the wall, some twenty years ago.'

'Twenty *years*? Then what the hell are *we* doing here? The murderer is long gone. Dead, for all we know.'

'That could very well be true, my lords.'

Askham ruffled. '"Could very well be true, my lords",' he imitated in a sour tone. 'Harken, Woodcock,' he said, elbowing toward his companion, who shied away from Askham's brusque movements. 'This is where Guest offers his services, stealing coin from the king's purse.'

These men meant nothing to Crispin, and he well knew he shouldn't be affronted at their rudeness, but it still riled him. He straightened; his chin raised. 'I wouldn't think of charging the office of the sheriff,' he said, turning slightly away. 'It's nothing to me. But Nigellus Cobmartin is an acquaintance of mine and I wouldn't dream of leaving him alone with it.'

'Who is Cobmartin?' asked Askham, swinging his head about like a snorting bull.

Nigellus timidly raised a hand and cleared his throat. 'My Lord Sheriff. I am Nigellus Cobmartin, barrister. And Master Guest here was kind enough to attend me when I sought out his advice.'

'Was he now?' Askham aimed his bulk at Crispin for only a moment before deferring to his companion. 'What do you think of this, Woodcock? Some sort of conspiracy?'

'I haven't the least idea,' he snorted, glancing longingly toward the door. 'It seems more for the coroner than for us. Mere bones. What can be made of that?'

Askham cast a reluctant glance up the long staircase, and Crispin could imagine the man struggling to drag his bulk up those many steps.

'Be at ease, my lords. The coroner has been called and will be here anon. If you don't wish to trouble yourself with such an old history of a homicide, then there is no need.'

'You're certain it is murder? You are always looking to make coin off the gullible citizens of London.'

'I am certain, my lords. He could hardly have coshed himself in the head, tied up his hands and feet, gagged himself, and proceeded to plaster himself within the wall. Unless you'd like to take a look yourself . . .' He gestured toward the stairs.

'No need to be overdramatic, Guest. No, I think it best we leave it for the coroner. There's little for us to do here. We'll leave the serjeants to await him and do his bidding. Oh. I suppose, Guest, it's too much to ask if you know who the unfortunate is?'

'Of course, my lords. His name is Wilfrid Roke. He was a varlet here for Master Cobmartin's father, deceased.'

'So, you have all the answers, eh, Guest? Very well. You may attend the coroner, then.' He took another last look around. 'I'll be glad for the end of this month. I'll wager you will too, Woodcock. For some other unfortunates to be appointed sheriffs in our stead.'

Woodcock said nothing either way. He glanced wearily toward the door.

Askham swept his cloak about him with a flourish and spun on his heel. Sheriff Woodcock was not as garish in his departure. He merely turned away from everyone without taking leave and stomped after Askham.

'That's us told,' said Jack once they'd gone, a lopsided smile tilting his mouth.

'I need not tell you, Nigellus,' said Crispin, 'that it is a great boon that the sheriffs will *not* interfere. For more often than not, they are a hindrance in getting to the meat of the matter.'

'How well I know it,' said Nigellus, seeming to relax from the encounter. 'Do neither of these appointed sheriffs ever take their charge seriously?'

'Very few, in my experience. But then again, they are mere keepers of the peace, with other vocations to look after. It would be better should the sheriffs actually be appointed to do the task I am paid to do.'

'Yes, wouldn't it.' Nigellus had a flicker in his eyes. 'An interesting notion. I wonder if you could petition the king—'

Crispin couldn't help an explosive snort of laughter. 'That would go very well, wouldn't it? Me, petitioning the king?'

'Oh, but King Richard is much more at ease these days, now that he has a new queen.'

'A child of nine that he does not see, away in her palace as she is. It will take some years before Queen Isabella comes to court.'

'I merely suggest that he is in a better mood these days.' But when he looked at Crispin's expression his brows rose in question. 'Isn't he?'

'Not if the rumors I have heard are true. Do you recall the lords who forced Richard to adhere to his kingly duties and keep his hands off the purse strings some years ago? Chief among them were the king's cousin, Henry Bolingbroke and Richard's uncle Gloucester. Richard successfully sent them all away, but he recently imprisoned his uncle in Calais for treason . . . where he mysteriously died. Do you not remember the outcry amongst the populace *that* engendered? It was assumed Richard's agents were sent to do the deed. No, Nigellus, it's best we all keep a low profile where King Richard is concerned.'

'Dear, dear. I suppose it completely slipped my mind, what with my brother and this house. Will you be all right?'

'Thank God and his mercy that Richard never thinks of me. But I do worry over Henry. I mean . . . His Grace, the Duke of Hereford. For he was also chief of the counselor lords and I fear Richard will go after him as well.'

'His own cousin,' said Nigellus.

'He had his own uncle murdered.'

'*Jesu* mercy.' Nigellus crossed himself. 'What a cross to bear it is to be the King of England.'

'Of course,' said Crispin, looking for any spies in the corridor or up the stairs. 'It is only a rumor.'

'That's . . . horrendous,' said Christopher. 'And you knew all those people, didn't you, Master Crispin?'

'Yes. I—'

'And just who is this charming boy again, Master Guest?' said Rykener, looking from him to Crispin with narrowing eyes.

'I'm Christopher Walcote,' the boy answered. 'I'm a mercer. My father, Clarence Walcote, is well-known throughout London. And Master Guest . . . was acquainted with my mother, Philippa.'

'I should say so,' muttered Rykener under his breath, giving Crispin widened eyes.

Crispin frowned. 'He's helping.'

'Oh, indeed,' said Rykener, smoothing out his gown. 'We all need as much help as we can get.'

'That's right,' said an oblivious Nigellus. 'Now that the records of that year are gone, we shall have to reconstruct the events as best I can remember them, as well as from those we talk to.'

'And I can see if any of those servants from those days are employed elsewhere in London,' said Christopher.

Everyone turned to stare at Young Walcote.

He smiled. 'I have connections. The mercer's guild is powerful and reaches all corners of London. I'm certain I can cast a wide net.'

Though somewhat stunned, Crispin tried to keep it out of his face. 'That's . . . very enterprising of you, Christopher.'

The boy rocked on his heels, his thumbs fitted into his belt . . . a gesture Crispin often used. 'Yes, I thought so, too. See? I *can* help.'

'Then go to it now. We'll either be here or at my lodgings.'

He saluted, trotted to the entry, and passed through the doors.

Silence fell as the company harbored their own thoughts. Until Rykener piped up with, 'Crispin. That boy. He bears a remarkable resemblance to—'

'We have to question the servants,' Crispin interrupted, feeling his face heat. He pushed past Rykener and headed back toward the parlor. 'Nigellus,' he called over his shoulder, and the barrister and Jack followed on his heels. 'Draw up a list of the servants and make note of who has worked here the longest. And then we shall see them one by one.'

'Would it not be better to see them all at once?'

'No. I want to hear their story as I ask it, not a corroboration of what they hear from each other.'

'Oh, very wise, very wise. *Audi et discerne.*' Nigellus scurried off to his own workroom near the steward's offices, but before Crispin could return to the parlor, Rykener slipped his arm into Crispin's, and leaned in close. 'Tell me, Master Guest,' he said quietly as they walked in slow and measured steps conducted by Rykener's stride. 'Tell me about this unusual boy, Christopher Walcote.'

Frowning, Crispin glanced down at Rykener's arm in his. He would not make a fuss in the man's own household. 'His mother was a client of mine some years ago.'

'Some . . . fifteen, *sixteen* years ago?'

'Thereabouts.'

'Crispin, Crispin, Crispin . . .'

'John!' he rasped. 'Whatever is bubbling in that mind of yours needs its lid firmly fixed upon it, just as I keep my counsel on how I address *you* in this household. It is a danger to his reputation should you spout out loud . . .' he glanced around, '. . . what you seem to want to say.'

'So I see.' Rykener sighed. 'Crispin, I would never endanger that boy. You must know that.'

Crispin huffed a breath. He conceded with a nod of his head.

John gazed at him tenderly. 'You must be proud of him. He seems so clever. Does he know . . .'

'Yes. And he has kept his counsel as well. The stakes are high, as you can imagine.'

Rykener shook his head. His eyes seemed to glisten. 'I find that so very sad. He obviously dotes on you. I don't suppose his, er, father, Master Walcote, is an ogre.'

'No, he is not,' he said reluctantly, and then he was ashamed of his tone, that he should have hoped that the man was a monster. 'He is a fine gentleman and none the wiser.'

'Oh, dear me. Well, it's for the best, then, isn't it?'

'Yes, for the best.' He turned to Rykener once they were inside the empty parlor. 'You will keep silent, won't you, John? I wouldn't for the world destroy his chances for happiness. It is my own folly that allows him to visit me.'

'And track with you.' He put his hand on Crispin's cheek. 'Dear Crispin. I don't blame you one bit. If I had a son – which isn't likely – I should like to keep him close to me as well. I'll keep silent. On my oath.'

'And Nigellus?' He gently pulled John's hand away.

'Oh, my dear Crispin. Nigellus is such a precious soul. I'm

certain he hasn't noticed at all. And never will. You know how he is.'

That was certainly true. But even if he had, Crispin depended on his natural discretion as a lawyer.

He surveyed the room. He drew a large chair with arms into the middle of the chamber. 'I find,' he said, as John looked on while he dragged the chair, scraping across the floor, 'that a certain setting is conducive to the application of interrogation.' Once it was situated as he liked it, facing the door and any who entered, he sat. 'Putting the questioned ill at ease in a subordinate position can significantly help an enquiry.'

'Why Crispin Guest. You are, at heart, a mummer.'

He settled in the chair, hands curling over the carved ends of the chair arms. 'Perhaps. Observe for yourself how the servants react.'

It wasn't long until Nigellus entered with a partial list and had the first servant enter. As the man slipped through the door, he pulled up short with Crispin sitting upright in that chair like a throne and pulled so far into the room that there was barely space for the servant to enter past the doorway.

'Who are you?' boomed Crispin, taking the list Nigellus handed him over his shoulder. He looked it over, not truly reading it, simply waiting for the young man to answer.

The man pulled his hat from his head and crushed it in his hands. 'I'm . . . I'm Martin, the stableman, m'lord.'

'Martin. Do you know what has transpired in this house?'

The youth, with spotted nose and forehead, and dry lips that he licked, glanced around the room at the faces he wasn't familiar with – at Jack standing stiffly to the side like a palace guard; at Crispin who must have seemed like Doom itself – and took a deep breath. 'They f-found a dead man. In the walls.'

'You're very young, Martin. You weren't here when the man Wilfrid Roke was killed twenty years ago. Now think, boy.' Crispin leaned forward, resting his arm on his thigh. 'Think very carefully. Do you know anyone who had anything to do with his disappearance? Have you heard anyone mention anything about those events of so long ago?'

'No, m'lord,' he answered immediately. 'I'm just the stableman. No one talks to me. Not much, they don't. I never knew there was a scandal until I heard tell of it today.'

'Have you ever been in the steward's rooms?'

'No, sir. Never.'

Crispin sat back, steepling his fingers. 'Where were you half an hour ago?'

'Mucking out the stables, sir. As I am usually doing.'

And smelled like it too, thought Crispin, getting a whiff of the boy. 'Very well. You may go.'

He bowed and scrambled so quickly out the door that Jack gave a little huff of a laugh. When Crispin glanced at him, Jack smiled. 'You do know how to frighten, don't you?' said Jack.

'There was a time when I frightened you.'

'Up until I realized for m'self that you didn't mean it.' He grinned.

Crispin angled toward the door, ignoring his remark. 'We'd best hurry. Send in the next one.'

The gardener, Rafe Hemm, entered, brushing down his patched tunic. His dark beard was thick and bushy around his chin and cheeks. He wore his rimmed hat low over his brow and he only flicked a glance once at Crispin before lowering his face.

'Hemm, you've been in the employ of the Cobmartin household for fifteen years, is that right?'

'Aye, my lord. Fifteen faithful years. I done naught wrong.'

'Keep to yourself, do you? Working the gardens?'

'I get the work done.'

'How often do you come into the house?'

He looked down at his hands. They were lined with dirt, the fingernails especially so. 'Not often,' he admitted. 'Only to get instructions on this and that. Master Augustus wanted the garden one way, and Madam Cobmartin insists on another way.'

'They don't come out to you.'

'Never, sir. That wouldn't be proper.'

'And so you come in to get their instructions on the garden.'

'Aye, sir. There's been a lot of coming and going with the house under construction. Men treading all over me flowers.'

Crispin studied his crusted shoes. He didn't recall any mud or dirt tracked into the steward's chamber.

'Where were you, just half an hour ago?'

'Digging up the garden path. With all the men going to and fro, I reckoned I needed to widen it. So as not to disturb the bulbs.'

'The bulbs?'

'Aye. The plantings. Madam Cobmartin will want her flowers.'

'Anyone see you there?'

He rubbed his nose with a dirty finger. 'Don't know. Could be workmen did.'

'Very well. You may go.'

'Thank you, my lord.' He bowed and hurried out, sending the next one in.

She was a maid – comely with a flirtatious air, blonde hair tucked under her kerchief. Her cheeks were rosy as if she'd rubbed them with blossoms, and her figure was rounded in all the right places. Unlike the others, she didn't seem frightened or shy. Just curious as to the goings-on, and looking over Crispin as if he were Christmas dinner.

He resettled himself in his seat. 'You are Jenna.'

She curtseyed. 'Aye, my lord.'

'You're a chambermaid.'

'Aye. I see to the bed chambers, that all are clean, that the pots are emptied, that the herbs are left in the room so that all is fragrant. And I see to the linens. It's a big job. There's only me, since Susannah only tends to Madam Cobmartin. She don't want to help with the other work. Puts on airs, she does. Not me. I'll do any work my masters want. That's the sign of a loyal servant.' Her head was angled downward, but she looked up at him through her lashes.

Crispin leaned forward in spite of himself. Jenna was a charming girl – charms that would be lost on her master, Nigellus. 'Are you a good girl, Jenna? Doing your prayers and devotions?'

'Oh, aye, sir. Master Cobmartin, that is, the *late* Master Cobmartin, was a devout man. He wanted the rooms just so. And Master Cobmartin – the present one – though he isn't as meticulous, he's such a good master. And Madam Cobmartin, too. She's good to me. They ask after me all the time.'

'And you wouldn't want the household to be torn apart, now would you? You wouldn't want your masters to be unhappy.

And they'd be unhappy if you were to help a very bad person, someone who would shield a murderer.'

Her cheeks blushed and her face opened in shock. 'No, my lord! I'd never. I'd never let anything like that happen. On my oath, sir!'

'Good. Where were you half an hour ago?'

'Airing out the master's chamber. Replacing the linens.'

'Did anyone see you at your task?'

'I don't know, sir. Maybe Susannah, though you can never find the girl when you want her. But . . . there are workmen about.'

'I see. Off with you, then.'

She curtseyed, and even in her distress, cast Crispin a last glance full of promise of rewards should he care to ask her again in a more private setting.

Or was he just imagining things? When he glanced at Tucker, the man was smirking at him.

Susannah came in next. Sauntered in, more like, thought Crispin. She did seem to have an air about her. She was round and pink-cheeked, but her dark eyes wandered all about the room. And she was wearing a gown that didn't seem to quite fit her.

'And who are you?' asked Crispin.

'I'm Susannah, Madam Cobmartin's personal maid.' She swayed, pivoting on her feet, flapping her skirts from side to side.

'I understand you are new to the household.'

'That's right, sir. Madam Cobmartin brought me here to cater to her.'

'Are you aware of what has transpired?'

She shook her head. She seemed bored of the proceedings. Her attitude didn't endear her to him and he leaned forward, face the blackest he could muster. It didn't seem to flap her. 'You don't know that a dead man was found within the walls of this very house?'

'Oh, *that*! Oh, aye.'

'It doesn't seem to trouble you.'

'Master, I've seen a lot. I've no need to get flustered at every happenstance.'

'Such uninterest could make one feel you might be culpable.'

'Of a murder that happened a generation ago? That'd be a

good one since I would have been two years old when I murdered the churl.'

Crispin sat back, scowling. 'Where were you half an hour ago?'

'Fetching fabric for new clothes.' She looked down at her gown, lifting the skirts to show him. 'The madam said I was to have new gowns. She didn't like this one.'

'You haven't known the Cobmartins long?'

'I've known madam for a long time indeed.' She said it with a sly tilt to her mouth and a glance toward John, and by that Crispin surmised where she had come from and the nature of her position.

'So I see,' he said, sitting back again. 'You may go, then.'

She offered a half-curtsey and was quickly gone.

'Who's next?' asked Crispin.

'It's the footman,' said Jack, reading the name off the parchment in Crispin's hand over his shoulder. 'Michael Loscroft.'

'Send him in.'

Jack walked to the doorway and motioned to someone.

A man entered. He was in his middle years, with dark, curly hair. He walked softly and with gravity, as if sensing just how his comportment should be in this instance.

'You are the footman, Michael Loscroft?' asked Crispin, steepling his fingers and staring at him down his nose.

'Yes, my lord,' he said with a bow.

'How long have you been employed in this household?'

'Well, a good long time. I should say sixteen, seventeen years now.'

'Had *you* heard of this tale of Wilfrid Roke?'

'I . . . I knew him, sir.'

Crispin leaned forward. 'You *knew* him? How?'

He pulled at his collar before smoothing down his cote-hardie. 'I was a servant to a mercer nearby. It was by chance at a tavern that I met Master Roke long before I acquired my position here.'

'You befriended him?'

'Not as such, sir. We just got to talking, as men do.'

'What did you talk of?'

'Oh . . . this and that. The day-to-day work that each of us did.'

Crispin waited, merely glaring at the man.

'Of . . . of our household matters and such.'

Crispin sat back and unsheathed his dagger, toying with it. 'What did you think of him?'

Loscroft's eyes followed the dagger. 'He worked in a fine house. Finer than my employers'. He held an honored position. I didn't think more of him than that.'

The blade caught the light and shone back on Loscroft's face. He blinked at it.

'How did you acquire this job?'

'I was looking for a better position than I had. I knew one of the maids and I applied to the master, the elder Cobmartin.'

'And he took you on?'

'No, sir. He thought I was impudent for asking.'

Crispin bared his teeth. 'Were you?'

He lowered his face. 'I suppose I was.'

'Then how came you here at last?'

'It was the mistress of the house. She was doing her shopping with a maid, and I saw two knaves following them. They were well-known on the streets as troublemakers. So I followed them all and, true enough, they made their move when the women had come to an alley. But I was there with my dagger and scared them off. She was grateful and asked me what boon I desired. I asked for the job of footman . . . and she granted it on the spot.'

'What did Master Cobmartin say to that?'

'He . . . he was grateful his wife was unharmed.'

Crispin glared at him for a few moments. 'Where were you half an hour ago?'

'At my duties, Master Guest.'

'Did anyone see you "at your duties"?'

'I don't know.'

Crispin measured the man one last time before dismissing him.

'That's not exactly how *I* recall it,' said Nigellus.

'Oh?' Crispin swiveled in his seat to face him. 'What do you recall?'

'Father was furious. He felt that Michael had somehow circumvented his wishes. He even went so far as to speculate that Michael had arranged for those men to attack my mother, just so he could be a hero in her eyes.'

Jack whistled. 'He said that?'

'Words to that effect.'

'Then why keep the man on?' asked Crispin.

'Because he didn't want to seem ungrateful in front of everyone. He proved – after a time – that he wasn't a schemer or a thief. Father even spoke highly of him in the years following.'

Crispin grunted a reply. He felt the same suspicions upon hearing the tale. But there was little to do but keep going with his investigations for the rest of the morning. Men and women of the household, and even the temporary workmen who marched through the door, encountered Crispin with frightened faces, and all claimed that they had nothing to do with any of the circumstances. And not one of them seemed to be hiding anything.

John Rykener threw up his hands. 'Well! That was a fruitless exercise.'

'Not necessarily,' said Crispin, rising from the chair. He stretched his spine, heard it crack. 'Jack, you were taking mental notes, no doubt.'

Jack straightened. 'Aye, sir.'

'Then let us to Nigellus's chamber and write down where everyone was at what time. We might ferret out who could have come into the steward's workroom before we got there.'

They returned to the ground floor and to a small chamber not unlike the steward's small space. Crispin little wondered why Nigellus had such a humble room, for the man didn't have grand ideas and it likely never occurred to him that he could well choose one of the rooms on the first floor near his own bedchamber.

It was as crowded with books and scrolls as the steward's chamber, and there was barely enough room for them all to squeeze into.

Jack shuffled through and perched upon the stool at the tall desk, grabbing parchment and pen. He gripped the quill little better than he had as a child, but his hand had significantly improved since those first frustrating days. He dipped, scraped off the excess into the ink pot and bent toward the leaf. Crispin peered over his shoulder as Jack sketched the Cobmartin manor house, with notations as to what room was what. 'Now then,' he said, crouching over the table.

'According to the nine servants we interviewed – including the steward's wife – they were approximately . . . here, here, and here.' He wrote their occupations rather than their names in the appropriate places: the maid in the master's chamber, the cook and the one scullion in the kitchens out in the back garden, the footman with the workmen – ten or so of them – on the first floor, the steward the same, the stableman in the stables, and the gardener in the garden working on the garden path, and even Susannah on the street. 'You see. Unless someone here is lying – and they most assuredly are – then no one was near the steward's room with enough time to get in it – assuming they had a key, and whereby St Paul's garters could they have got one? They'd have to get in, find the scrolls – also assuming they could find them—'

'They'd have to be able to read,' said Crispin.

'Right, sir. They'd have to, wouldn't they? Master Nigellus, who amongst your servants can read?'

'Well now.' He put a hand to his shaven chin and rubbed. 'The steward, of course. William. The cook, the footman . . . who else?'

'The gardener and the stableman,' put in Rykener.

'You have a very literate household,' said Crispin.

'Yes, we do,' said Nigellus thoughtfully. 'My father and I . . . well. It was our indulgence that we wanted them to at least have a rudimentary knowledge. It is helpful, you see, for the running of a house. For ordering supplies and . . . such.' But he must have realized while saying so that it meant that there was a wider expanse of suspects. He released a frustrated sigh.

'Well, at any rate,' Jack went on, 'the culprit would have to get in here, find the scrolls, burn them sufficiently so they could slip out again and back to their place, and not get found out.'

Crispin leaned an arm on the desk and scanned the names in their positions. 'You've left someone out.'

Jack wore an indignant expression. 'Who, sir?'

'William Roke. We didn't place him.'

'Yes?'

Everyone turned toward the doorway. Roke himself stood there, discomfort flitting over his features.

FIVE

'A timely arrival,' said Crispin, straightening.

'Oh. Well, I had only just remembered something and thought it might be helpful.'

'I'm listening.'

Roke scanned all the faces staring at him. 'I was only a child, you will recall. But I remember there being shouting and loud voices before my mother died. I remember a time when my father stormed into our room, my mother's and mine. I was playing on the floor. "You're behaving disgracefully!" he yelled at her. "What if I am?" she shouted back. And then I became frightened at their loud voices and I climbed out of the window and into the gardens. I could hear them still shouting as I left them behind. There was a trellis covered in vines and I used to hide there when the servants or others were angry with me or each other. It was a good place to hide. There was a burrow, you see, from some rabbit or badger. No one could find me there if I did not want to be found.'

He finished speaking and had the look of a man who realized he might have said too much. He shuffled and looked down at his feet. 'I don't know whether it is helpful or not.'

'Do you know what that disagreement was about?' asked Crispin.

'I don't. Does a child ever truly know what the adults around him are saying?'

'A fair point. Do you recall your parents often having such loud disagreements?'

'It seemed so. But that might just be the memory of a child. I seem to remember . . .' But he stopped, frowning.

'You were saying, Master Roke?'

'Oh. It's just that . . . she and Master Justin also argued. My mother. Not loudly, but in hushed whispers. I came upon them once in a window alcove in the gallery.'

'Master Justin the former steward?'

'Yes, before Master Philip. My father was also antagonistic to him. And to the *other* man.'

'What other man?'

'Another. I think he was a workman. But I'm not certain. I don't think he was a permanent part of the household, but I saw him a great deal. At least for a while.'

'A workman?'

'Yes. When Master Cobmartin senior was enlarging the north wing.'

'A *workman*,' Jack said significantly to Crispin. One who would know how to plaster a wall.

'Your father argued with him as well?'

'Yes. I saw him at the top of the gallery once, pointing his finger right into his face, and his own face was twisted in anger.'

'But this is extraordinary,' said Nigellus, shaking his head. 'Wilfrid was known to be very accommodating, very mild-mannered.'

'Begging your pardon, Master Nigellus,' said Jack, 'but that was his servant face. What I mean is you'd act differently to your betters than you would to your equal. The servants' hall can be . . . well. Sometimes you kept yourself armed at all times.'

Crispin stared at him. 'Truly?'

'Aye, sir. Not you and me, mind you. But in other houses. Just like lords would act with each other, and not in front of the Duke of Lancaster, for example. Like that, sir.'

'Just so,' said William. 'A servant must act with a mild manner to his master or he will find himself without a master at all. That is well known.'

'Well. My education has been lacking then,' said Crispin, thinking. But he did recall his days at court, and yes, his fellow peers would have a more generous comportment with the kings and earls than they would among themselves. He supposed it was to be expected in the servants' hall as well. After all, there was a hierarchy among the servants as there was at court. The lowest of the household – the scullion, he supposed – had no one to lord over but their own children.

'I concede it,' he said finally, giving a nod. 'Wilfrid's animosity toward his fellow servants might be the cause of his murder. You can only have so many harsh words for a man before he turns on you. But William,' Crispin gathered his thoughts before carefully asking, 'how did your mother die?'

'She broke her neck, so they said. Falling down the stairs.'

'The stairs in the foyer?'

'Yes. They are wide, you see. Standing in the middle as they are. No railing to catch yourself if you stumble. I've stumbled on them many a time.'

Crispin flashed back to his own mother who had died the same way, and how he'd been the only one to find her for what seemed like hours. She had still been alive, and he had held her hand as she died, the life leaving her eyes.

He cleared his throat and the dusty memories with it. 'I see. Where were you nearly an hour ago, before we arrived?'

'Me? I was . . . let me see. I was in these rooms, trying to straighten them.' He held open his arms in a gesture of futility.

The room, however, was only steps away from the steward's.

'Jack, don't you have something for Master Roke?'

Jack's face was a blank before his eyes widened in remembrance, and he reached for his pouch. 'Oh aye! Here, Master Roke.'

He pulled out the leather cord with the cross with the jewel and handed it over.

William took it and stared at it. 'What is this?'

'I took it from your father's . . . from your father. I thought you might want it.'

'Oh. Indeed. It's . . . just that . . .'

'What is it, Roke?' asked Crispin.

'It's just that . . .' He slumped. 'I don't remember this. It's a sad thing not to remember your sire except for his yelling.'

'You were young. Surely you can't be expected to recall every memory.'

He turned it over and over in his hands. 'It was his. That's all that matters.' He clutched it tight in his fist. 'Thank you for this, sir.' He bowed to Jack. 'Is there anything more you want of me?'

'No, Roke. That's all for now.'

They watched him leave, and as soon as he had, Crispin

turned quickly to Jack. 'He could have burned the scrolls. He could be protecting someone.'

'Someone who might be dead. The old steward?'

'Yes. Dammit. If only we knew what those scrolls said.'

Nigellus rubbed his hands in a nervous gesture. 'The death of his mother troubles me.'

'Yes,' said Crispin. 'This so-called mild-mannered man might have had a temper and he might have pushed her down the stairs.'

'It's horrible to contemplate,' said Nigellus. 'But I have tried many a case where a husband had done worse. Cruel, cruel things have been done to men's wives. I shouldn't say it, but I am glad they were all hanged.'

'Not your clients, I hope,' said Crispin.

'What a tangled tale,' Rykener lamented, striding through the small room, sunlight on his shoulders. 'Such things happening all around the Cobmartin family, and none the wiser.'

Crispin nodded, eyes absently roving over the books and parchments. 'But the servants would know.' He flicked a glance at Jack. 'The servants always know.'

Jack nodded.

'I'll need to talk to that cook again. Still. It's a diabolical and carefully planned murder. Might the cook know of this "other man", this workman?'

Jack blew out a breath and scrubbed at his ginger curls. 'Nothing for it but to ask him.'

'Yes,' said Crispin. 'I can't help but think we are missing something crucial.'

'Shall we call him forth again?' asked Nigellus.

'No. Jack and I shall go to him.'

'Oh.' Nigellus looked to Rykener and Crispin offered them a smile.

'You may get back to your own work. Jack and I are on the trail.'

'Didn't I tell you, Nigellus?' said Rykener, rushing to the man and grasping his hand. 'I told you we needed Crispin Guest. He'll solve it.'

Crispin had his doubts, but he said nothing as he ushered Jack out of the room. 'How are we ever going to solve this one, master?'

'I don't know, Jack.' He strode over the tiled floor before pushing the heavy door to the back courtyard open. 'We might get lucky. But it seems – with so many passing years – that it might prove impossible.' They walked through a garden, its last vegetables and herbs bravely clinging to dying vines. He passed a fragrant trimmed ball of rosemary before stepping onto a stone path that led to the kitchen building. The garden seemed deader and less cared-for than it should have been, he thought on second glance. He didn't recall his gardens looking this poorly when he had his estates in Sheen.

'But I don't like not finding justice for the victims,' he said.

'Poor Master Roke.' Jack made it to the door first, grasped the iron ring, and hauled it open, allowing Crispin to stride through first. 'I can't even imagine what he might be thinking. He might never know who killed him.'

'Pray that we will find some answers.'

'I always do, sir.'

Another archway and they passed through to the kitchen. It was smaller than Crispin expected, but after all, even as big a house as it was, there were few inhabiting it. Two masters and ten servants. Crispin's old estates were four times the size and there were three times as many servants . . . and all for a single lord: him.

The cook and scullion were there, preparing the dinner. They did not notice Crispin's or Jack's presence at first. They stood there a while, watching the furious work of cook and servant. Until the scullion whipped about and plunged toward a shelf only to be blocked by the two of them. He let out a yelp that made the cook turn from his bubbling kettles over the fire.

'Master Guest!' he said, brandishing a long spoon like a weapon.

'Master Robert. I had some additional questions.'

He grumbled and clutched the spoon. 'Well then? The kitchens are a busy place.'

'Forgive my intrusion. But do you recall when Wilfrid Roke was the varlet here if he had many loud disagreements with his wife?'

His indignity at being interrupted deflated. He lowered the spoon and put his hand to his chin. 'Well now. If I do recall at all . . . yes. Especially those last months before she . . . before she died.'

Crispin stepped closer and spoke more quietly. 'Master Robert, do you believe there is any possibility that Madam Roke might have died from . . . misadventure?'

The cook glanced back at the scullion busy chopping vegetables. 'There was no proof, mind you. But I have to say, it did cross the minds of the servants here at the time.'

'Did no one talk to the sheriffs or the coroner?'

'We all thought . . . well, if the sheriffs or coroner did not bring it up, then there was naught to it.'

Crispin kept his growl to himself. How many crimes had gone unpunished because those who might have been witnesses were afraid to come forth? 'Would you have characterized Wilfrid Roke as "mild-mannered"?'

'He was a good man, good at his work. No one had a harsh word to say about him. He could be jealous of his wife, however.'

'Had he cause to be?'

'Rumors, Master Guest. But rumors can be fatal.'

'*Were* they fatal in her case?'

The cook's brows lowered over his eyes. 'I have never voiced that opinion. But it was possible. Anything is possible. But it was so long ago.'

'And yet you seem to remember it well.'

The man shrugged.

'Do you recall any servant or workman who seemed to pay Madam Roke particular interest?'

Robert narrowed his eyes in thought. 'Well . . . now that I think on it, there was one man. Mind you, the work was extensive, building a whole wing as they did. So the workmen were present for some years. I seem to recall one man in particular. Dark-haired, he was, and handsome. Everyone remarked on it. What was his name? Thomas. Yes, Thomas was his name.'

'And his surname?'

'That is much harder to dredge up from the past, Master Guest. Let me think on it. But he was London born. His people were from Friday Street.' He chuckled. 'Funny that I should recall that and not the knave's name.'

'Names can be harder to remember,' said Crispin. 'When it

was assumed Wilfrid Roke ran away with the household relic, what did you think of that?'

'I was shocked. Everyone was. He took to his vocation sincerely. No one could imagine what got into his head.'

'Yet it might have turned out not to be the case.'

'Yes.' He tilted his head upward and stared into the rafters. 'I suppose . . . I am gratified that it wasn't so in the end. What I mean to say is . . .' He rubbed his calloused hand up and down his white beard-stubbled cheek. 'I'm not happy he's dead, mind you – the saints bless him – but I'd be happier knowing he was no thief. Was he a thief, Master Guest?'

'It is too early to tell. What of the missing maid at the time? Ardath?'

'Once we thought Wilfrid had made off, we assumed again that it was to meet with her.'

'Is she alive today, in London?'

He shook his head. 'I don't know, Master Guest. Never heard a word about her since.'

'I thank you, Master Robert. I shall not interrupt you again.'

'I will think on the workman's surname.' He ran his other hand up the spoon's shaft. 'I didn't mean to be surly to you, sir. It's just it's busy in the kitchens. But I would see someone pay for poor Wilfrid's death.'

Crispin nodded to him in dismissal and motioned to Jack as they left the kitchens. Outside in the garden, Crispin paused. 'I believed him,' he said, gazing at the borders of thinning blooms and carefully coifed trees.

'I do, too, master. It's as I reckoned.'

'Yes. It's going to be damnably hard to find any further clues. Why don't you walk the grounds for a while longer with your list? I'll take my leave now and make my way back home. But, er, don't look for me too soon.'

'Aye, master,' he said, cocking his head.

Crispin left the garden and retreated through the house. He looked for Nigellus or John, but not seeing them, he left without word.

The fact of the matter was standing in the kitchens made him think of scullions and of one in particular from so long ago.

Philippa Walcote had been a scullion in her master's house, and had risen in ranks to marry him, though the first Master Walcote turned out to be an imposter. She married the brother of the one he was impersonating, but not after first asking *Crispin* to marry *her*. He had cursed himself hundreds of times over the years for turning her down. He hadn't known he would spend a decade and more mourning that decision.

And so he naturally found himself on Mercery looking up at the Walcote manor house, with its gatehouse and walls around it. The trees were larger since the last time he'd been there. He had studiously avoided the street, tried not to be reminded, though he saw Christopher enough.

He had no intention of going to the gatehouse where the porter sat under the arched portico. But a voice behind him startled him almost to the point where he drew his blade. It was a good thing he hadn't.

'Philippa! I mean . . . Madam Walcote.'

She was alone as was her habit. Other ladies in London had escorts, but she was still too much of a kitchen wench to demand one. And she was smirking at him. For there was only one reason for his being there, and that was to catch a glimpse of her. 'How do you fare?' she said in her lowborn accent. For years she had tried to cultivate a more palace accent, but it was only in the last few years she had given it up. Her husband Clarence didn't seem to mind, nor her associates.

He finally remembered to bow in greeting, and was exasperated with himself that she had caught him out.

'Will you come in, Crispin?'

'Oh . . . I don't wish to trouble you . . .'

'Clarence is out of town on business.' She said it with a wink. 'Come in for some ale. Or wine if you prefer. And you can tell me where Christopher has got up to. I swear by all the saints that he spends more time with you on the Shambles than he does here.'

She strode forward nearly across the lane before pausing to look back. 'Well, come along!'

He knew he shouldn't – her husband was out of town, after all – but in the end, he couldn't refuse. He followed her. The porter acknowledged his mistress with a nod and barely a glance at Crispin. Many people of various types must have passed through that portal over the years.

They entered through the main entrance and then he continued to follow her to the ground-floor parlor. No servants accosted them to take her cloak, and none were in waiting to serve the ale.

She must have noted his concern as he glanced about. 'Clarence likes to be waited upon. I do not.' He should have guessed it. She was used to taking care of all on her own, including the business. Clarence might have been the mercer, but it was likely that Philippa took care of the day-to-day running of the business itself; the warehouses, the accounting. She had learned it well from her first husband, the imposter Nicholas Walcote.

She stood at the sideboard and poured ale into two goblets, turned, and handed him one. She was a little plumper than she used to be, but it didn't detract from her charm and delectability. If anything, her cheeks were rosier, her smile brighter. Her hair was still that brassy gold, plaited into two buns on either side of her head and encaged in gold netting and a light veil. With her cote-hardie of embroidered French serge, his eyes easily followed all the curves and dips of the fabric clinging to her form.

He decided he was staring and turned to the room instead. It was the same, with its colorful tapestry, amusing wall mural of dyers frolicking around their vividly colored vats. A sideboard with bas relief carvings of people and more dyers stood guard on the other side of the room, where she had used the silver wine flagon and ornate goblets. She had all the riches, all the trappings a woman could desire. But somehow, Crispin thought that it was Christopher that mattered the most to her than all the silver goblets in the world.

She watched him curiously as she made her way to the hearth, grabbed an iron rod, and poked it until the flames reached higher. She sat with a long exhale and drank a hearty dose of her cup. 'Don't just stand there,' she said, gesturing toward the other chair.

He stood like a fool, staring into his goblet, and wondering how he had allowed himself to be in this position. He glanced up when she laughed.

'I've never seen you look so jumpy before. The great Crispin Guest, Tracker of London!' She saluted with her cup and drank again.

'Forgive me, madam,' he said, embarrassed. 'But your husband is out of town and . . .'

'Do you think I will leap upon you and ravish you?' She giggled over the rim of her goblet. Those eyes. Their heavy-lidded gaze never failed to make him lose his composure. To hide it, he walked to the opposite chair and sat.

'There,' he said, slightly angry with himself. 'I'm sitting.'

'Oh, don't growl at me. Here we are old friends. We should be able to jaw a bit.'

'We are more than old friends, Philippa. God's blood, you know that!'

She slowly sank back, still holding the goblet nearly to her lips. 'I know,' she said softly. 'There's that oath that so endeared me. "God's blood." Do you know Christopher says it now?' She took a sip and set the goblet aside on a table. 'Tell me how you are. Truly. I would know.'

He sighed before shrugging. He put the goblet on a side table without drinking. 'I am well. Jack and I are doing very well indeed. Better than we have in years. We have two horses, a goat, and chickens.'

'Horses? I am gratified to hear that.'

'And . . . Jack's children. I am . . .' He couldn't help but smile, shaking his head. He felt his face heat with a blush. 'They seem to dote on me. I am equally enamored of them. It's . . . very different.'

She smiled and offered a gaze full of warmth. 'Tell me.'

'It is strange. Oh, I suppose I doted on Henry, Lancaster's son. I enjoyed his company and helped raise him along with his many governors. But this is different. Little children, babes, all around me all the time. I suppose they view me as an uncle of sorts.' He settled in his chair, unconscious of getting more comfortable as he talked. 'Whenever I return home, they run at me, giving me hugs, telling me all the adventures they'd had that day. When I was a lord, I never would have got close like that to servants' children.'

'See what you missed.'

He looked up at her as if coming out of a dream. 'Yes. Yes, I do see that.'

They gazed at one another for a long silent span. He took up the cup and drank while she sipped from hers. The fire crackled and warmed them, and they merely sat in the comfortable silence together. 'I suppose,' he said after a time, 'it would have been like this. You and I.'

She sighed. 'Have you found no one, Crispin? After all this time?'

'A couple of years ago, I did ask a woman to marry me.'

She sat up, setting her goblet aside. With hands clasped – rather tightly, he thought – she studied him. 'And what happened?'

'We weren't in love, but I thought it would be mutually beneficial. She didn't see it that way. She . . . *she* was afraid of soiling my reputation with her rather notorious one.'

Philippa sat back again, head leaning against the chair. 'She rejected you for *her* reputation?'

'The irony did not escape me.' He set his cup aside once more. 'I shall never marry. I'm too old now.'

'Your Lancaster married his long-time lover and he is ten years older than you.'

'They'd been together all this time. I was glad when they finally married. I was glad Richard allowed them to.'

'But you won't allow yourself to.'

'Philippa,' he said with a sigh. 'I fear there was only one woman for me. A love I failed to see at the time.'

'But there is a greater love even than that. You love your suffering.'

He glared. 'I beg your pardon?'

'Don't give *me* that look, Crispin Guest. You're so used to playing the martyr that you find it difficult to stop.'

He only glared harder. He felt the anger bubbling in his gut.

'You were banished from court, and how long did it take for you to come to terms with your fate? You were sour about it when I met you and you were seven years from court then. And over the years you kept your lot like a burning coal inside of you, letting it fester away at you. Until Jack Tucker finally put out that coal. And now you say, "I shall never marry!"' She imitated his palace accent and tone before she laughed. 'Poor Crispin. Poor, sorry knight. Why won't you forgive yourself and live? Find a wife. Then we can at last sit together, like we are now, and smooth away the roughness of the past. I should like to be your friend, not your ghost.'

The anger, like the burning coal she described, suddenly extinguished and he stared into the hearth, watching other ghosts dart and jump in the flames. He took a breath. Then another. 'There is . . . much wisdom to what you say. But I am who I am, Philippa.'

'I know,' she said, and they were silent for another long interval, a comfortable interval, he had to admit, until she turned to Crispin. She clasped her hands together and pressed them to her chest as she suddenly leaned toward him. 'What do you think of Christopher?'

He felt the tense muscles in his shoulders soften again. 'I am very proud of him. You've taken excellent care of him and his schooling. I couldn't have asked for more.'

'He's learnt so many things from you. I'm glad of it.' She frowned. 'Here now, in't he supposed to be with you now?'

'He was. I am currently investigating a crime . . . a murder from twenty years ago.'

'Twenty years ago? How is that possible to discover?'

'It won't be easy. Christopher is . . . helping.'

She said nothing for a long time, but her eyes were narrowing as he realized what he'd said. He snatched up the goblet and drank.

'You have my son solving crimes with you?' The gaiety in her tone had left her.

'He . . . he begged to go with me.'

'And you let him? He could be in danger.'

Crispin jumped to his feet and paced before the fire. 'He wanted to go. And I . . . I in my foolishness . . . wanted it too. I'm sorry. When he returns to my lodgings, I will tell him he must return home.'

'You'll do nothing of the sort.'

He froze, afraid to move. He couldn't make out her expression. Was she angry? Irritated?

And then she laughed again, a raucous, merry sound. 'You

should see your face. You would think a cloud of doom was descending upon you.'

'It very well could be,' he muttered.

'Crispin . . .' She rose and stood before him, much too close. 'I am pleased that he wishes to work with you, as long as it don't interfere with his studies or his work here. He's a clever boy with a quick wit. I've no doubt he'd be as good as you at tracking. But he will be a mercer.'

There was no mistaking her tone. In the end it was still about money and status. She didn't want her son to be a poor man like Crispin. Even though she had said the opposite when she had asked to marry him all those years ago. All he could offer her was his poverty . . . and his love. But *he* couldn't stomach offering any of it to a scullion. Not then.

She, however, had learned that lesson well.

He turned away with the intention of leaving. Being in her presence was too tempting for him. It was one thing to think about her in the dead of night in his bedchamber, and another indeed to stand before her.

She caught his arm. He could have easily wrenched away, but he didn't.

'Philippa,' he said softly in admonishment. At least it was meant to be a rebuke. Instead, it came out a soft caress, the way he would have wanted to say it had they been alone in a more intimate setting.

'Crispin.' The way she said his name caused the blood to surge within him. He didn't remember turning abruptly, or even grasping her shoulders to pull her in. All he knew was the shape and feel of her lips as he kissed her, the heat of her breasts pressed against him, the thudding of both their hearts.

'Why?' she breathed. 'Why can I not forget you? I long to be your friend.'

His arms encircled her, keeping her close as he kissed her deeply. She yielded to him with a sigh and held him just as tightly. 'I wish . . . I wish I *could* stop loving you,' he whispered to her throat.

'You're too stubborn,' she said with a deep chuckle.

'As are you.' It made her laugh again, and he gloried in the sound of it pressed against him. He bent his head to take her lips again, breathing her breath, tasting as she tasted him.

But when he finally withdrew and held her away from him just enough to gaze at her, the sensation of their mutual affections slowly drained away. They both wanted each other, that much was plain by her moistened lips, her eyes seeking his. But they both knew it was impossible. Crispin loved her and she loved him, but neither wished to cuckold the man who was father to Christopher, who was a gentle and true husband.

His fingers still clutched at her arms but he gently pushed her away from him.

'If only we could turn back the clock,' he said softly.

'If only,' she said with a sad smile.

The door opened and Crispin startled. The figure – a servant, likely – stood in the doorway for a long moment before Philippa looked up and gasped.

'What is this?' said Christopher with an unsteady voice . . . and with a hand on his dagger hilt.

SIX

'**M**other?'

In that instance, Crispin heard the child in his voice. Crispin turned to face him and to shield Philippa. 'Your mother is innocent. It is I who forced my attentions on her. I apologize to you and to her.'

The boy's hurt expression stabbed at his heart.

Christopher didn't draw his dagger, but he breathed hard and suddenly spun out of the room. Philippa moved to go to him, but Crispin grabbed her arm. 'No. I'll go.'

'He will be angry with you.'

'Better me than you. I fear . . . this is the end of his visits to me. And . . . this is the end of my visits to you.'

'You speak as if we do this with frequency. Faith, Master Guest. It has been years.'

'I know. But he won't believe that.' He kept her hand in his for as long as he could have it, gazing at her face, until he finally let her go.

He raced into the foyer and spied an open door out to the garden. He followed it and stepped outside, glancing about. And there, under a tree and sitting on a bench, was the boy, face encased in his hands, elbows on his thighs.

Crispin approached carefully, but the boy never looked up, even when he softly said, 'Christopher.'

'You don't belong here, Master Guest.'

'No. I most assuredly do not. And I will not return.'

The boy didn't move his face, but his gray eyes flicked upward between his fingers to look Crispin over. 'Are you laying with her?'

'No.'

He drew his hands away from his face. 'Are you lying to me?'

'No. I swear by God's gracious heart.'

'Hmm,' said the boy, looking away.

'We kissed, but that was all. We . . . God's blood.' He ran a hand down his sweaty face. 'I . . . I love your mother. I have never stopped loving her since first falling for her some sixteen years ago. But we have not . . . we *will* not commit adultery. We both respect your father too much for that.'

He leaned back against the tree behind the bench, letting his arms flop to his thighs. 'And does she love you?'

'I . . . I don't know. She did once. She is a good and true wife to your father. You must never think otherwise. I was the one at fault.'

'You believe that, don't you?'

'Because it is the truth. I have no business being here. It is her kindness and generosity to me that I have trod upon. I should never have entered your home. And I shall not again.'

The boy lay his head back and breathed hard into the ether. 'Why must it all be so complicated? I love the both of you, *and* my father. Why must . . . why must . . .'

'Life is very complicated, Christopher. Mine, perhaps, the most complicated. I would not entangle you in my life or bring my grief to your household. And it's probably best that you don't visit me again.'

He shook his head. 'But I don't want to stop seeing you.'

'And . . . I don't want to stop seeing you. But we must. Don't you see? The older you get . . .'

'The more I look like you. And someone will say so.'

'Yes. You see the difficulty.'

'Do you think . . . my father would disown me?'

'I don't know. I'm not willing to take that chance.'

'Isn't it up to me to make that choice?'

'No, dammit! Your mother married Clarence Walcote to have a better life. She didn't know she was already with child. She . . . wanted the best life for *you*. Don't you see?'

'I understand. I love him, too. He's always been a kind father. Funny, loving. I can't see that he'd be cruel. But . . . I can also see that he might have to be. He . . . he can't let them laugh at him.'

'No, he can't. And we can do him a service and keep it from happening.'

'If I don't see you anymore.'

Crispin nodded. He'd tried to hold off that lump in his throat but it was no use. That hot thickness was there, stinging his eyes. 'And so I should take my leave now. I am sorry, Christopher. God keep you. Be well.'

He turned just in time before his eyesight began to shimmer and his lip trembled. There seemed no end to his disgrace, no punishment left off the list. He'd have to forget he had a son. It was the only way.

He strode hard through the gatehouse, down Mercery Lane toward the Shambles. He made the turn at Gutter Lane and stalked a straight course for the Boar's Tusk.

When he sat in his usual corner facing the door, Gilbert the tavern owner seemed to sense his mood and simply left the jug of ale and a wooden cup. Crispin poured, drank, poured, drank, and sat back.

The smoky room seemed crowded with the shadows of many figures, or was it that he didn't care to see who was there in the haze? But he smelled the familiar hearth, the fragrant ales, the sweating men and damp floors, and felt reasonably satisfied.

Yes, he'd finally done the honorable thing, after *not* doing the honorable thing by kissing Philippa. He didn't know if he wouldn't have gone further. He'd wanted to. God, how he had wanted to! He didn't know whether he was angrier at himself for going to her in the first place, or for getting caught by Christopher. But he knew it was all his fault. Damn all of it to Hell.

He tipped the jug over the cup again and sloshed some of the beer onto the table. He drank only a little this time. He didn't want to fall into *all* his bad habits of the past.

He stared into his cup a long time before someone flopped down next to him on a stool. He rather suspected it was Jack Tucker, and so didn't look up until he spoke.

His twisted round when he saw that it was Christopher.

'You didn't let me finish,' he said before he took the cup from Crispin's hand and drank it down. He took up the jug, looked inside, and poured more into the cup. 'What I was going to say, before you left so abruptly, is that your decision to bar me from seeing you was out of the question. I have too many things yet to learn from you.'

'Christopher. You must know how foolish this is—'

'You keep interrupting me, Master Guest. This will never work between us if you keep on interrupting me.' He drank again before setting down the cup. 'I don't want to get drunk.' He belched. 'My mother won't be best pleased if I come home at the end of the evening stinking of ale.'

'Master Walcote,' Crispin began with a growl.

'Ooh, "Master Walcote", is it? Now I know I'm in trouble.'

'No, *you* are not in trouble.'

'So you want all the trouble for yourself? That seems very selfish.'

It was all getting muddled in his mind. How much had he drunk? But he didn't feel tipsy. He gestured to Christopher, pointing a finger at him. 'Harken to me, boy. I don't know what foolishness you are concocting in your head, but I want you to stay away from me. Do you understand? It's for your own good.'

Christopher pulled at a loose string on his sleeve, seemed preoccupied with it as he spoke. 'So many people over the years have told me what is for my own good. My tutors, my father's journeymen, my mother, my nursemaid, my governor . . . If it's all for my own sarding good, shouldn't I enjoy it more?'

'Language,' muttered Crispin without thinking.

'And that's another thing.' He slammed his hand to the table. 'God's blood! I can swear if I want to. I'm almost a man.'

'But not yet.'

'*Your* problem is you don't understand the youth of today. We want to have our own say.'

Crispin swung in his seat. 'What was that nonsense you just said to me?' asked Crispin, brows digging into his eyes.

'You don't understand the youth. I'm not Jack Tucker, you know. I'm younger even than him. Me and my peers, we talk about it a lot. How the aldermen of this city run things. We don't like it.'

Crispin was suddenly struck dumb. The . . . the *gall*. The utter gall of the lad. Who did he think he was?

'I can't believe what I'm hearing. And what does this have to do with—'

'All I'm saying, Master Guest, is that I'm my own man. That I make my own decisions. And someday *I'll* be an alderman and fix the ills of London. It's not like it was when you were my age.'

'Oh, isn't it?'

'No, it isn't.' He paused and seemed to gird himself. 'And though it's true that I was . . . disturbed . . . by catching you and my mother—'

'We only kissed,' he rasped, keeping his voice down.

'I know that. And I was angry and disappointed and . . . and frightened. Not for myself, but for my mother. I would not have her sin.'

Crispin finally lowered his face. 'Neither would I.'

'You see? You *are* a man of honor. And that is what I wish to be. Who better to tutor me?'

'Your father!'

'No, he's busy with this and that. But you. You understand the ways of the world better than most men. *That's* what I would learn. That's what you excel at.'

'God's blood, boy. Didn't you hear one word I said to you?'

'Yes, I heard it all. It was the speech of a most chivalrous knight. Where am I to learn that?'

A spark of hope he had no right to feel warmed his chest.

This boy – this too-clever-for-his-boots boy – had found an argument that Crispin found difficult to cross. Well, who was he fooling? He grasped at it like the last tree limb hanging over a cliff.

'You are far too clever for yourself, boy.'

'And who did I get that from, I wonder?' he said quietly.

Crispin gave him a sidelong look. He suddenly wanted to laugh. He never thought to meet a man as clever as Jack Tucker, who could twist logic all around him and weave it into its own reason. But here he was.

'Christopher,' he said after a long moment of contemplation, 'if you can forgive me for taking liberties, I can accept our continued friendship. For all the good it will do the both of us. God willing, we will not destroy your life in the doing of it.'

Christopher's serious expression gave way to a wide grin. 'Alleluia! You're finally talking sense.' He put his hand out to shake and Crispin reluctantly took it. 'Now, as to my other news—'

'Ho, Crispin!' came a shout from across the room. Crispin looked up and scanned the many faces in the crowded space, until he saw a man in cassock waving to him. He rose and greeted the man halfway to him with a bow.

'Abbot William. What are you doing here?' They clasped hands and Crispin pulled him along to their table.

'Is that any way to greet an old friend? I haven't seen you in many a day, Crispin. You owe me a game of chess, remember?' The old abbot – a man who looked more like a merchant with a wide face and light blue eyes than a nobleman – glanced at Crispin's companion. 'Well, now. Who is this young man? A relation of yours, Crispin? By the Rood, he looks just like you.'

Crispin grabbed the abbot and yanked him down to a seat. 'You don't wish to awake the whole tavern with loud conversation, do you, my lord?' he rasped.

The abbot stared at him and leaned forward to rub at his backside.

'This is Christopher Walcote,' said Crispin, gesturing to the boy, 'the son of the prosperous mercer, Clarence Walcote. Christopher, this is Abbot William de Colchester, of Westminster Abbey.'

'A very great pleasure, my lord,' said Christopher with a respectful bow.

Abbot William was still staring accusingly at Crispin, and Crispin tried to appease him by pouring ale into the cup on hand and pushing it toward the cleric. 'Some ale, my lord? All I meant by way of greeting was that this tavern is so far from the abbey. Not that you had no cause to be anywhere in London you wished to be.'

'Well . . . I . . .' He glanced once again at Christopher before giving his attention to Crispin. 'I had some business in London . . . and I was thirsty . . .'

'Then drink up. I am glad to see you. I did not mean to imply that I was not.'

'You're friends with the Abbot of Westminster Abbey?' said Christopher, shaking his head. 'I don't know why at this juncture I am surprised by any of your friendships.'

'Now you, young man,' said the abbot, leaning over the small table and clutching his cup. 'You say you are a mercer? You aren't related to this knave Guest?'

'I am interested in his vocation.'

Well parried, Christopher, thought Crispin.

'Why, my Lord Abbot,' Christopher continued, 'just today, Master Guest has been engaged in investigating a twenty-year-old murder; a murdered man's skeleton plastered *inside* a wall of a house. Isn't that intriguing?'

'Bless me,' said the abbot, crossing himself.

Crispin leaned on the table as well. 'Indeed. A vexing case.'

'But how should it be done, Crispin? I know you are clever, but surely even you have your limitations. Something that happened so long ago.'

'I admit, there are many problems associated with it. But each piece is a puzzle to be worked out.'

'So you have said many a time. Are you aware, young man,' he offered, gesturing with his cup, 'that this man has cracked some of the deepest puzzles of murder? Something no one else could have done, I'll wager. I know your mind is keen, Crispin, but I owe it to the gifts of the Almighty. That He watches over your deeds and rewards you with insight.'

Crispin bowed. 'It must be so, my lord. For it is sometimes

a bolt from the blue that gives me a notion. For instance—'

'We discovered that there was a varlet that everyone in the household believed had stolen a relic and run off,' Christopher interrupted, words coming fast in his eagerness. 'And for twenty years, his memory was vilified. Can you imagine it? Your good name dragged through the mud.'

The abbot flicked a glance at Crispin. Crispin could imagine it well.

'And then,' Christopher went on, heedless, 'all at once, your bones are discovered, and it's revealed that *you* weren't the villain, but some other, who had murdered you and blamed you for the theft for all these years. And there you were: bound, gagged, and entombed with the relic.'

'Good God.' The abbot crossed himself again and looked from one to the other of them. 'Your friend here, Crispin, seems as keen as you are in solving these puzzles. Perhaps you might have found yourself another apprentice.'

'I don't think Jack would like that,' said Crispin.

'Oh, I'm to be a mercer,' said Christopher, matter-of-factly. 'Like my father.'

'It is good for a man to follow in one's father's footsteps. I, of course, did not, for my calling was higher. In any case . . . this reminds me of something from long ago. Another servant in another household. He, too, was thought to be a thief, and he too was murdered. Bless me. I haven't thought of this tale in many years. He was a valued man, trusted by one and all. But the object was missing – I can't even rightly recall what it was now – and the man was gone. When a thing is presented in such a way, why . . . you don't question it. The servant was gone and so was the object so it was natural to assume. There was no one in the house to naysay it. With the evidence of their own eyes . . .'

Crispin nodded. 'As you say, Lord Abbot. Why assume anything else other than what is in front of your face?'

'But not you, Crispin.' He took a drink and gestured to the boy. 'Maybe you are not aware, Master Walcote, but our Crispin here always sees what is beyond the awareness of his eyes. You wait. Something amazing will come to him, by the Lord's intervention, of course, and he will have puzzled it out. You wait, my boy. Patience, in the case of Master Guest, is indeed a virtue to be most prized.'

'You flatter me, my lord. The puzzles only seem to grow harder the older I get.'

Abbot William smiled. 'I doubt that.' He pushed the cup away and rose. 'Well, I must go. I've tarried long enough. I only wanted to greet you and to remind you to come to the abbey. You mustn't neglect your friends.'

'I was just telling Master Guest that same thing,' said Christopher, studiously *not* looking at Crispin as he said it.

They both rose and walked with the abbot out of the door. Christopher held the abbot's horse steady as the older man mounted.

'Farewell, Crispin. And may God bless you and speed you on your course. I know that He watches over you.' He sketched a benediction in the air over him, and Crispin bowed to accept it. 'And farewell to you, Young Walcote. If I didn't know better, I would call you father and son.' He tapped the horse's flanks and moved into the street. Crispin pulled his hood up, shielding his face from the people who stopped along the street to watch the abbot ride slowly down the lane.

Christopher lowered his face as well, but he could not seem to scrub away his amusement. 'Your friends, Crispin.'

'They're very *loud*,' he muttered.

'I liked your abbot very much, but his appearance interrupted me as to what I was going to tell you.' He postured, thumbs in his belt. 'Guess what I found out? The missing maid from twenty years ago? Ardath? I found her.'

SEVEN

'I . . . I am astounded,' said Crispin. 'How did you?'

'By thinking like you,' he said, thumbs in his belt. 'I talked to several mercers who sent me to others to talk to, and on down the line. She's still alive.'

'Is she?'

'Yes. Shall we go to talk to her?'

Crispin couldn't help smiling. 'I reckon we should.'

They started walking toward Billingsgate. He couldn't seem to stop stealing glances at his son, while Christopher, no doubt knowing Crispin was doing so, simply smirked, pleased with himself.

A cart piled high with faggots caught their interest, and they both watched it silently creak and sway through the mud before it turned a corner, leaning far enough that it might have tipped . . . but didn't. 'Funny about Madam Roke falling down the stairs,' said Christopher abruptly, after the cart's squeaking dimmed into the distance.

'Funny? How?'

'Oh, well. I just heard from the other lads in the guild. It's one of those *accidents*,' he said with a wink.

'You mean foul play.'

'Yes. It seems when a man tires of his wife, she often falls down the stairs.'

'So by this, you infer that Master Roke tired of his wife and she had a misadventure down the Cobmartin staircase?'

'It's possible.'

'It is. It might interest you to know that Jack and I have been contemplating that very notion.' After a pause, he added, 'My mother fell down the stairs . . . and died. I was there. I was six.'

He caught the boy's expression out of the corner of his eye. The gray eyes were wide, mouth gawping like a carp.

'What . . . what happened?'

'It *was* an accident.'

'But . . . Master Crispin. What if it weren't?'

'Don't be ridiculous. Of course it was an accident.'

'But how do you know? You were only six.'

'Well . . . because I . . . because . . .' He furrowed his brows. How *did* he know? He went by what the others had told him. But his father wasn't home at the time. He was seldom home. And then *he* died anyway in battle several months later, without ever returning. Crispin couldn't quite remember what either of them looked like.

'She was my grandmother,' he heard beside him. The boy's

voice was awed and then he turned toward Crispin with a raw expression. 'She was my grandmother,' he said more distinctly. 'I suppose she was.'

'I . . . I don't know much about you. Not truly. I don't know where you lived and who you knew and the things you've done.'

Crispin rolled his shoulders. He had been afraid of this. As the boy grew, he'd want to know more about his heritage, a heritage long gone.

'Can you tell me about her?' said Christopher. 'About my . . . about your mother?'

Crispin sighed. There was a dull ache from behind his heart. He supposed they were old memories trying to breach the careful walls he'd constructed over the years. 'I don't remember much of her. But . . . she was kind and sweet . . . and somewhat sad. Perhaps because her children had died some years before.'

'You had siblings? They'd have been my aunts and uncles.'

'They were children when they died. I am the lone survivor.'

The lad cocked his head. 'Funny you putting it like that.'

'I suppose I heard it put to me like that enough that I absorbed the expression. My father died not too long after my mother and that's when I went to live in the Duke of Lancaster's household.'

'You were a page at six?'

'Yes. I was very studious. I . . . loved living in that household. I learned everything I needed in order to become a knight and lord. I had my own estates, you see. In Sheen. I inherited all but had to learn the means to run it properly, care for my tenants. It is not enough to be wealthy. One must learn one's responsibilities.'

'*For to each man to whom much is given, much shall be asked of him; and they shall ask more of him, to whom they betook much.* I remember you telling me that. I took it to heart.'

'I am gratified that my words of wisdom have not fallen on deaf ears.'

'I've listened to everything you've ever told me.'

God's blood, he thought. He mustn't allow this. He mustn't allow the boy this hero-worship. 'Christopher, if I were so wise at everything, I would not be in the position I am in today. I would have been a lord, doing as I should have done, not eking out a living on the streets of London as a tracker. I'm glad that you have minded me where it counts, but I am a fallible man. Certainly Clarence Walcote has qualities to emulate.'

Christopher frowned and turned away toward the street. 'Just because I admire you doesn't mean I've ignored him. He is my father in every sense. I'm not a fool.'

Falling silent on the matter seemed the better course, Crispin decided, though he longed to say more.

But the silence between them was broken when Christopher suddenly asked, 'What were the names of your siblings?'

So much for the boy's speeches. Still, he couldn't fault him for wanting to know of his bloodline. 'Well, first there was Henry, then Robert, then Joan. They all died before I was born.'

'I'm sorry.'

He bit his lip. 'I am too. My parents are mere memories to me. Like a dream. Like . . . leaves on the wind. I can't quite capture their faces anymore. I know how William Roke feels.'

'They'd be proud of you.'

He huffed a laugh. 'I very much doubt that. I was a traitor, boy. You must never forget that. It meant that the family name was struck from the rolls of knights and lords. And it was my fault. The lone survivor.' He spat the last.

'But you couldn't have known . . .'

Crispin stopped, passed his hand over his face. 'Look, Christopher. What I did was wrong. I swore oaths and then I broke them. An honorable man must never do that. He must never forswear his oaths to his lords, most of all. And this I did. The king is the king, anointed by God. Who was I to undo what God has made?'

'You thought it was the right thing?'

'What fancies you weave.' He strode out into the mud again. 'Who have you been talking to?'

'My mother,' he said quietly.

Crispin closed his lips. There was nothing more in this world that he'd rather do than talk of Philippa . . . except to hold her in his arms. But he pointedly said nothing.

After another short pause, Christopher asked, 'The Cobmartins. How did you know them?'

'I met Master Cobmartin when he was defending me . . . at my trial for murder.'

Christopher's mouth fell agape.

'He was successful . . . obviously. And then he became my landlord, the place we now live.'

'Oh. And what about . . . about . . . M-madam Cobmartin?'

'John Rykener, you mean.'

'Yes. Yes, he likes going about in women's clothes. Does he think he *is* a woman?'

'No. But John has had a difficult life, though he makes light of it. He is . . . or was . . . a whore.'

He let Christopher stew on that for a bit, working it out.

'He was also one of the kindest men I ever met. For when I was first thrust into my new life far from court, I didn't know what to do, where to live, how to earn money. None of that was I ever required to do as a knight of the court. But back then, I was like a babe in arms, wholly innocent and desperate. John was kind enough to take me in. His compassion is the greatest thing about him, to be sure.'

'I'm glad he did that for you. I shall defend him with my last breath for his kindness.'

Crispin smiled and patted Christopher on the back. 'Kindness to one's fellow man should always be rewarded but seldom is. I . . . I never approved of John's ways, nor his situation now.'

'You mean . . . pretending to be the wife of Nigellus?'

'Yes. John takes it very seriously, I'm certain.'

'But, how can they? They are two men.'

'There are ways and ways we know not of, Christopher. Even the scriptures speak of David and Jonathan. *I make sorrow upon thee, my brother Jonathan, full fair and amiable more than the love of women.* Perhaps it is thus with them. It is not for me to understand.'

Christopher fell silent within his own thoughts, and said nothing more as he led them down a narrow street to Billingsgate and to a tall, wide shop there. Above the door, it had the sign of a scissors. A tailor, then.

Christopher walked up to the door and knocked smartly, stepping back with his hands behind his back. When the door opened, a man similar in age to Crispin with a well-fashioned russet cote-hardie answered and looked them both over. 'Yes?'

'Are you Master Cleve?' asked Christopher.

The man stared at Christopher, but saved an extra-long stare for Crispin before he answered. 'I am.'

'Is your wife at home, sir?'

'Say, what is this about?' He moved into the doorway as if guarding the gates of a castle.

'Sir,' said Crispin, nudging the boy aside. 'I am the Tracker of London, Crispin Guest. We would speak to your wife with regards to an unpleasantness with her former employer.'

'Former employer? My Ardath has been my wife these twenty years now. Former employer!'

Crispin folded his arms over his chest and raised his chin. 'We will await her.'

That seemed to startle him into action. He stepped into the darkened interior, leaving the door ajar. Crispin stepped up into the threshold and pushed the door wider to walk in.

'Master Crispin,' hissed the boy.

'Don't stand in the street,' he admonished without turning round. He scanned the room with its bolts of cloth carefully piled onto shelves; the large table with its sharp shears and chalk; a leather cylinder containing pins. It was a neat shop, fairly clean, with the makings of a cote-hardie on a manikin of linen, with pins stuck in it to keep the pieces of the coat together on the torso. The room smelled pleasantly of cloth and dyes.

Christopher inspected some of the bolts, taking the cloth between his fingers and rubbing them, then passing his hands down the weave. Christopher nodded, seeming to approve. The bolts had tin buttons pinned to the fabric, proving the taxes for them had been paid. Perhaps some were Walcote cloth. At least the boy was learning his trade.

A woman in her middle years came down the steps, followed by the man who had opened the door. The hair poking from her kerchief was blonde touched by silver. She was slender, with a willowy way about her, but a frown kept her features from being something Crispin might call pretty.

'What's this, then? Who wants to see me?'

Crispin offered an abbreviated bow. 'I am Crispin Guest,

madam, Tracker of London. I am enquiring about the days you worked in the Cobmartin household.'

'So my husband said. Whatever could the matter be? It was so long ago.'

'Indeed it was. But something has come to light that makes enquiries urgent. You left that household with nary a word.'

'That's not true. I told the madam. And a maid. And then I left.'

'And why did you leave?'

'Here,' said Master Cleve. 'What's this got to do with aught? That was twenty years ago.'

'Master Cleve, it may very well have to do with murder.'

She gasped and clutched her husband's sleeve. 'Murder,' she breathed. 'Whose?'

'Do you recall a Wilfrid Roke?'

'Wilfrid? Aye. He was Master Cobmartin's varlet, was he not?'

'He was. Do you recall the instance of his leaving the household?'

'Oh, aye,' she said, her hand over her mouth. 'It was right before I left,' she said to her husband. 'Before we wed.'

'Wasn't that the churl who ran off with the household relic? I recall you telling me that.'

'Aye, that's the one. Why have you come to me?'

'The circumstance of your leaving about the same time—'

She shrieked and threw her hands up. 'Oi! You thought he and me . . . That's a chamber pot full, that is.'

'No one knew what had happened to you, madam. It was believed by some that you ran off with him.'

'Who, I'd like to know!' She rolled up a sleeve as if ready to strike the miscreant.

'Dearling,' said the husband, his hand gentle on her shoulder, 'it seems quite proper that one would think that. If they hadn't known.'

'But I told the madam.' She put her hand to her hip. 'No one knew, good sir?'

Crispin shook his head. 'They did not appear to. And those that remain to this day in the household did not know either.'

'But you said . . . murder.' She whispered the last.

'Indeed. Master Roke has been found. Murdered. With the

relic. He was bound and killed and left within the very walls of the manor house.'

Both Master and Madam Cleve stood with mouths agape, not a squeak between them. Until Ardath Cleve blinked and shook her head. 'And you thought that I'd done it?'

Crispin looked her over. She was too slight to have hauled the dead man into the wall. And would she have known how to plaster him in? But Cleve could have helped? Still, the question remained why?

'Do you have any idea why anyone should have done such a thing to Master Roke, not only murdering him, but making it look as if he stole the family relic and made off with it?'

'That's a sore thing, isn't it? I can't imagine. And I certainly didn't do it.'

'Was he a difficult man?'

'I never thought so.' Her fingers were at her mouth again. But her eyes were cast back to another time. 'He was kind and merry to the maids and the others. It was his wife he wasn't too kind to. Oh! I know I shouldn't speak ill of the dead. But it was a true fact, sir. He railed against her.'

'She fell down the stairs.'

'Aye. And there was much talk of that in the household, I can tell you.'

'You didn't believe it was an accident?'

'To tell you true, sir, I did not. I think she was ready to leave him.'

'Oh? Was there someone . . .'

She got in closer to Crispin. Master Cleve edged forward to hear, as his wife spoke quietly. 'There was a rumor. Only a rumor, mind. I don't think no one there knew for certain. But they thought she was going to run off with someone.'

'Any idea who?'

She shook her head mournfully. 'It was so long ago. I don't rightly know, sir.'

'Does the name Thomas jar any memories?'

'Oh! Aye, it does. There was a Thomas. And a right handsome man he was. I do recall her spending time with him. He was a stonemason, so I think. Fancy that. Thomas Courtney.'

'That was his name?'

'Aye. I'm fairly certain of it. Thomas Courtney. I haven't thought of that name in many a day. Dark-haired and handsome, he was.'

'You already said that,' said Master Cleve with a frown.

'I think many a maid tried to catch his eye. Certainly not me,' she said hastily to her husband. 'For I was enchanted by you, my young man.' She cast an adoring look to him. He seemed to melt under it.

'You've been very helpful,' said Crispin. 'Should you recall anything more, do not hesitate to send word to me on the Shambles at the old poulterer's. Anyone can point it out.'

'I shall. Let me think on it.'

Crispin bowed. 'Then, I bid you both good day.'

Christopher bowed to them and followed Crispin out.

On the street again, Crispin turned to Christopher. 'I am pleased that you chose to stay silent.'

'I thought I'd learn more from watching you. And learn I did!'

'Oh? And what, pray, *did* you learn?'

'I noticed how you walked a fine balance between a lordly demeanor and one of a tradesman. It put them at ease, but at the same time kept them on their toes.'

His brows flicked upward. 'That was very discriminating of you.'

'I doubt I would have been as keen if it had been someone else. I pay close attention to you . . . to see if I do the same things.' He offered a sheepish smile. 'Sorry.'

'No need to apologize. I, er, find myself studying you at times for the same reason.'

Christopher gave a nervous laugh. 'You do?'

'Yes. You do, you know. Have my same mannerisms. Strange that you should, having been raised by another.'

Christopher appeared amazed . . . and charmed. 'What? What is it I do?'

'I shan't tell you. It will only make you self-conscious of them.'

'Oh, come, Master Crispin! You must tell me now!'

'I don't think I will.' It was like a young Jack Tucker all over again. Crispin smirked all the way back to the Cobmartin manor.

EIGHT

Nigellus sat in a blade of sunlight, staring at the relic in his fingers. His office was stuffy and warm, perhaps almost warmer than he liked, and the books and parchments piled high on his shelves seemed to close in on him. He wasn't quite certain what disturbed him the most. Was it the specter of death hanging over them now? But many a man and woman died in their own houses. It was something devoutly prayed for, to die in one's own bed, after all.

But surely not in the walls.

The hard crystal felt smooth and cold in his fingers, and he rolled it over and over. He'd cleaned the chain, worried it had traces of the dead man, and wondered whether he should wear it as his father had done. But what good had it ever done *him*? Nigellus had talked once to Crispin Guest about such things, for the man seemed to stumble upon relics with a suspicious regularity. Guest was pragmatic about them, though, believing in the veracity of very few, and generally shied away from any form of veneration. He supposed he couldn't quite blame the man. After all, they always seemed to involve murder, at least those Guest came upon.

He raised the crystal close to his face and studied its foggy surface, the blurred curl of hair within. Guest had once told him that there was great enterprise in the selling of false relics. Was this just another one of those? Is that why it hadn't helped his father?

'Oh, there you are!'

He tried not to be startled by John's loud voice, but it was a useless effort in the end. Hiding the fact that he had jumped, he pretended deep contemplation of the relic . . . which, he supposed, wasn't pretense at all.

'I do have work to do, John.'

'And you seem to be hard at it.' Without so much as a by your leave, he snatched the relic from Nigellus's hand. 'What do you plan to do with this? It's rather horrible when you think of where it was found. I hope it offered the poor man some comfort in his last hours.'

'If he was aware, I'm certain it did.' He sighed. 'I was just contemplating that very thing. My father used to wear it.'

John made a face and handed it back. 'Won't it make you think of all the unpleasantness associated with it?'

'I don't know. It is a holy object. It must have seen great misery . . . as well as great joy.'

'Perhaps you should ask Crispin. God knows he's familiar with enough of them.'

'I was thinking that too.'

'Well. Let me see you with it, then.'

Nigellus paused before pulling the chain over his head and letting the relic rest on his chest. John cocked his head and looked at it first leaning to the right, then the left. 'You do look very proper with it, like a successful lawyer should look.'

'Do you truly think so?'

John smiled. 'You always look wonderful to me, my dear.' He leaned in and kissed him. Nigellus felt his face flush.

'Then . . . perhaps I *will* wear it. At least as a remembrance of my father.'

'You're right, of course.' He patted Nigellus's chest. 'Now I must go and talk to the cook. We simply cannot have another stew.'

'You can't go to the kitchens, John. It isn't proper. You must get a servant to bring Cook to you in the solar.'

John huffed a breath. 'That seems so unnecessary. Do you think I am better than that poor fellow who labors over the fires for us?'

'Well . . .'

'If you speak *one* word in agreement . . .!'

'I . . . wasn't going to,' he mumbled, even though he had been about to tell John that they *were* better than the cook, else *they'd* be cooks and scullions. But John came from a different life than Nigellus had. A whore was not better than a cook, surely. Yet, it was good for his soul, he decided, to put himself into the shoes of others, to cultivate more empathy. A lawyer should have empathy. After all, he wasn't a judge now, was he?

'Well . . . you must do what you think best, my love.' He always conceded to John. Why even bother to argue? And it made the man smile, which surely made it all worth it.

John flounced out of the room, leaving Nigellus in solitude again. He picked up the relic where it hung on his chest, studying it once more before he let it lie. He *must* get to his cases, or there wouldn't be any income to finish their house with.

Hours later, he was in deep contemplation of the parchments before him. Fingers into the points of his eyes, he squeezed his lids shut. The writing had gone blurry. Too much reading, not enough light. And no wonder. One of the candles had snuffed out. He took a straw from the metal cup by the hearth, lit the straw from one candle, and relit the other. And it was then he saw the shadow in the doorway.

A figure in silhouette hung there, not moving. It was not John, for it was in men's clothes by the shape of him, and not too tall either. A workman?

'You there! What do you want?'

'I beg your mercy, sir.' He stepped into the halo of candle and hearth and his face was finally recognizable. William Roke.

'Well, young man. What is it?'

'I didn't wish to disturb you, sir.' He seemed to be fumbling with the necklace Jack Tucker had taken off his father's body.

Nigellus smoothed his face and his ire at being interrupted, for this man surely felt the pain of all that had transpired. '*Ut in calceamenta aliquis ex*,' he muttered. Aloud, he said, 'There is something you wish to say? Come in, Master Roke. This has been quite a day.'

'Yes, sir.' He shuffled in and stood by the fire, looking around. 'I . . . I've always liked this room, sir, if you don't mind my saying. So many books and so . . . cozy . . . a space.'

Nigellus sat back, pleased. 'Yes, I could have a bigger room, I suppose. Perhaps I should . . . but I like it too. It's snug. It directs the mind to the work at hand. It's very like your clerk's room.'

'Oh yes, sir. And I do like that too. I feel that I do important work there.'

'And so you do. What can I do for you?'

'Well . . .' He looked down at the pendant, seeming surprised to find it in his hand again. He clutched it once and let it drop. 'I can't put my finger on it, sir, but something about my father's body disturbs me.'

'Naturally, the circumstances . . .'

'Yes, of course, but it isn't only that. But I can't seem to get my mind around it, if you know my meaning.'

'It was a long time ago.'

'It was. But . . . that's not quite it.'

'And you thought, perhaps, if we discussed it, it might come to you?'

'I don't know. I'm greatly disturbed by it. Relieved, too, that he wasn't a thief, but now disturbed that someone in this household hated him so much that he was murdered and in such a way.' He stepped closer. 'You've been to the King's Bench, haven't you, sir? You've met murderers and the like. Why did they do it?'

Nigellus nodded and rubbed his shaven chin. 'Yes, I see. Well, the murderers I have been acquainted with had some motive for their crimes. Usually it was money. But sometimes it was for the love of a woman. And still others in a sort of rage. You see, murder is described in the law in several ways. There is *murdrum*, a slaying done in secret as this one surely was. Then there is *simplex homicidrum*, a killing that was unplanned by accidental circumstances or in self-defense. And still others of *manslaughter*, the slaying in hot blood, as in a duel. But you must already know this, for you have written out my notes on these very instances.'

'I have. And I've wondered about them. I've been angry once or twice, but I would never have killed anyone, sir.'

'And I conjecture that most men would think thus. But there are those who cannot control their baser instincts. Men whose anger gets the better of them. *Ab incunabulis* for some men, I must presume. Ah, William.' He rested an avuncular hand on his shoulder. 'Do not vex yourself on it, for Crispin Guest will ferret it out. I have every confidence in his talents in this regard. And you must too. Pray for him.'

'I will, sir.' Again, he looked down at the pendant. 'And this. I'm glad I have something from my father.'

'You may find yourself remembering your parents more and

more. *Dabit illud tempus*. But don't hesitate to come to me if you are still vexed. I fear I have not been of much help to you.'

'Oh, no, sir! Your regard has been the best help. For I know that you care about these things. Especially in your own household.'

'Indeed, William. We will get to the bottom of it! Never fear that. Pray God gives us the strength and the wisdom to understand all that we find.'

'Amen,' he said, crossing himself. He offered a grateful smile before he left, clutching again at his cross.

Nigellus sat back with a sigh. He'd never been the head of a household before. He hadn't realized the time it would take out of his day, and the new role it meant. He was the father to all who inhabited the place, he supposed. They would come to him now with grievances and their sorrows as well as their joys. He never expected to be in such a position and yet he should have done. He had wanted to be a successful lawyer, after all. It had meant he'd have something of a grand house. Not as grand as this one, but still. And he was glad in the end that he had landed at last in his childhood home after all, even though that meant that Augustus was gone.

'Well, enough of this speculation. I must to my work.' He pulled the parchments from the top of his desk in front of him, and settled in. But try as he might, he could not manage to concentrate on his carefully penned words, nor on the notes made by William Roke in his very readable hand. He pushed them aside.

'My mind is not on it. Curse this murderer whomever he was.' Was he even alive? Would justice be served? What a dreadful thing to befall them all. He had noticed some workers leaving, not wishing to work under the onus of the death and whatever blackness that surrounded it, and he could hardly blame them.

A throbbing in the top of his head began again. This simply wouldn't do. He had to make the money in the family, for he dearly wanted John to cease all work that didn't involve embroidery. He needed more clients, more cases. And how was he to accomplish that if he couldn't even finish the ones he had?

He tried again, pulling the parchments toward him. He read,

scratched notes next to certain points of law that he questioned, but the headache would not abate. Perhaps if he went to Cook for something. Robert always had some sort of potion that he kept for the household.

He hopped off his chair and stretched his back. And maybe something warm to drink. He should just call a servant, but like John, he was used to getting things himself. He shook his head at the two of them. Alas, it was meant to be that he would have an unusual household.

As he strode into the entry, he once again heard the sawing and hammering of the workmen above. Since the body had been taken away, they had resumed their work as the steward Philip Able no doubt set them to doing. The man lived up to his name; he *was* an able steward, to be sure.

Nigellus could admire the other improvements as he walked down the corridor to the back of the house. This was all John's work. The man knew well how to coordinate colors to be best pleasing to the eye. After all, he used threads of various colors for his embroidery. He thanked the Almighty each day for John's presence in his life, even if they sinned by their living together in what the Church would consider an unnatural order. But it didn't feel unnatural. It felt quite natural and quite . . . well. He loved him. Though he did worry what God would think. Jesus did not seem to preach against such things. Nigellus had made very careful readings of the Sermon on the Mount. Even so, he dared not broach the subject in confession . . . which was itself a sin. He sighed.

It had honestly never occurred to him to love a man. He'd never been interested in women, not with his studies keeping him occupied. He would have obliged his father, he was certain, had he obtained the hand of a willing woman for marriage. But his father was just as preoccupied as Nigellus had been, and never bothered to find his son a wife.

He stopped to inspect a tapestry he had never seen before. It was small, perhaps two feet square. It could even have been something John had made. Nigellus wasn't very good at remembering things that John told him. It wasn't that he didn't want to pay attention, but he had so many things on his mind, and John did love to talk.

He wondered how long they could keep up their charade. Wasn't someone bound to notice? He hoped not. As long as they remembered to lock their chamber at night, he supposed they could keep it up indefinitely.

He opened the door to the garden and stood in the doorway, taking in how dead and weedy it was. Augustus hadn't taken good care of it, even with the gardener. But now with John cracking the whip, he could see small changes already – though it might take several seasons for it to return to the former glory his mother had created. John had the same sensibilities. He did have an eye for beauty, did his John.

Maybe he should dismiss this gardener. After all, the man had taken his salary under false pretenses. He clearly hadn't been doing his job. Though, in all fairness, if Augustus hadn't prodded the man – for his brother didn't care for things such as gardens – it was, in the end, Augustus's fault. Nigellus hated to confront people, even servants. And then he chuckled at himself. *Imagine a lawyer afraid to confront people*, he mused.

A breeze brought the smell of herbs wafting toward him. It truly would be a home after everything was put in order. Except for that pile of leaves under the trellis. It seemed out of place to the work the gardener was finally putting his back into. Nigellus wouldn't have noticed it had it not been for a ray of sunshine that lit the usually shadowed hollow. He supposed the gardener would soon get to it with his rake and wheelbarrow. Nigellus remembered that when he was small, he liked to watch the gardener work. That had been the old gardener who had a wispy gray beard and even hair in his nose and ears. Nigellus loved watching him swing his scythe and lay low the grass, then rake it up and carry it off. He had watched him trim the roses and all the flowers, laying straw beneath them in the wintertime and trimming them down to stubs, and it was a wonderment when they budded in the spring.

'Young Master Cobmartin, I wondered where you'd got off to,' the old man would say, and he'd welcomed Nigellus back and even let him trim the dead blooms himself with the old gardener's clippers. He'd had to use *two* hands. He had liked that old man but couldn't for the life of him remember his name now. *Was it Samuel? Sebastian? Something with an s.* He was long dead, he supposed. One day he was there, and the next time Nigellus was at home, the man was simply gone, and another gardener had taken his place. But that was when Nigellus had been fourteen or fifteen and off to Gray's Inn by then.

He walked along the path, the gravel crunching under his shoes, and the gentle rain of autumn leaves settling about him. He looked back at the dark patch of leaves under the trellis and stopped. He cocked his head as he looked at it, for it didn't seem quite right to him. Should he bother with it? Shouldn't he just get the gardener Rafe Hemm to remove it? It was his job, after all.

He was walking toward it before his mind could reckon he had done so. And when he stood looking down at it – the dark shape tucked under some berry bushes and covered by leaves – he realized it wasn't some garden trimmings at all. It was . . . it was . . .

'Holy saints. William! *William!*' He knelt and shook the boy's shoulder. He shook it harder but as he did so, he saw the dark beneath him like a crimson shadow.

'Help! Someone! Help! William is hurt!'

Workmen came running, servants ran forward from every-where, and John appeared from the kitchens throwing a hand over his mouth.

'Oh, Lord preserve us,' John whispered. 'We must send again for Crispin.'

'Yes,' said Nigellus. He had begun to tremble. He reached back for John's hand and clutched it hard. 'Dear Lord in Heaven. Dear, *dear* Holy Mother. It's another death.'

NINE

C rispin had arrived back to the Cobmartin household and before he could say a word, they hustled him to the back garden. He crouched over the body of the young man and shook his head in disbelief. Jack stooped alongside him.

'Blind me, Master Crispin,' he said quietly. 'Why, after so long, would the son of Wilfrid Roke have been attacked?'

'I can think of but one reason, Jack. Because the killer is still here.'

'But that can't be possible.'

Crispin glanced at Christopher standing stoically beside Nigellus.

'I'm afraid it is possible. And what's more, this can't be the end of the killings.'

Nigellus, who had been standing back next to John Rykener in his woman's clothes, dithered with his hands. 'What did you say, Master Guest? There's *more* danger to be had?'

'It's as if someone is trying to wipe out the memory of the Rokes. And the only two left who even knew them are the cook . . . and you.'

John grasped Nigellus so tightly the man squawked. Nigellus carefully disentangled himself from John. 'My God, what should we do?'

Crispin rose. 'You should leave this place. You and the cook.'

'For how long?'

'As long as it takes for me to find the killer.'

Nigellus put his fingers to his mouth. 'Dear me. This is a disaster.'

'Better that we found out now,' said Crispin, 'than after the fact.'

'After the fact!' squealed John. 'God in Heaven! We must pack at once!'

Nigellus turned to him, his face pale. 'But where would we go, my dear?'

'I don't care. Far from here. Back to Gray's Inn?'

'Yes, I do have lodgings there. But, er, they don't allow . . . females.'

'Nigellus! Don't be a silly fig. I'll change my clothes.'

Crispin sighed. It was out of his mouth before he could stop himself. 'Come to my lodgings when your luggage is prepared. You can change there.'

'Oh, Crispin!'

He stiffened as Rykener descended upon him and enclosed

him in a bone-shattering embrace. 'John,' he winced, 'I can't breathe.'

'Oh, sorry.' He stepped back, dusting down Crispin's cote-hardie.

'But what of Cook?' asked Nigellus.

Crispin felt a headache coming on. 'If he has no relatives, then, I suppose, he can lodge with me, as I fear there will be no privacy at Gray's Inn.'

He and Nigellus exchanged glances. The lawyer had one room there. And with John . . . how would he explain Rykener's presence?

The steward approached. 'Master Cobmartin . . . and Master Guest. The sheriffs are here.'

Nigellus placed a hand to the side of his face. 'Not again.'

'I'll deal with them,' said Crispin. 'You and . . . and Eleanor should pack. Very lightly.' He signaled for Jack to help them and Christopher followed.

The sheriffs turned at his approaching step and glared in his direction. 'My lords,' said Crispin with a deep bow. 'And so. Another murder.'

'Weren't getting paid enough, eh, Guest?' said Sheriff Askham. 'It's not by the body, is it?'

'I have no idea of your meaning, my lord. I am here assisting Master Cobmartin with his difficulties.'

'Right under your nose, Guest,' said Sheriff Woodcock, stalking toward him with hands tucked behind his back, and his nose jutting forward in the attitude of a common crow striding across a green.

'In fairness, I was pursuing another avenue of my investigation, and wasn't on the premises at the time.'

'Excuses he has by the penny,' tisked Askham, shaking his head. 'There's always an excuse, isn't there, Guest?'

'Obviously the investigation continues. But I have ordered Master and Madam Cobmartin from the premises, as well as the cook.'

'And what is the meaning of that, by all the saints?' asked Woodcock.

'Because, my Lord Sheriffs, they were the only members of the household who knew the first murdered man, and I fear for their safety. The original murderer is obviously still here among us.'

Askham fiddled with his chain of office and rested a gloved hand on his sword hilt. 'What foolery is this, Guest? The murder was twenty years ago. What makes you think this new one has aught to do with the other?'

'Because it is the murdered man's son who was slain. It can't be a coincidence.'

Woodcock sneered. 'I can lay bare hundreds of writs that show coincidences.'

Crispin said nothing. He merely stood as he was, waiting.

'It's damnable, is what it is.' Woodcock swung away from Crispin to go to the sideboard and pour himself some wine. 'Traipsing all over London to this same household. You're not doing your job, Guest.'

Only because you aren't doing yours, he huffed in his head. It would have been satisfying saying it aloud. At one time he might have. But he was getting too old to be brutalized by sheriffs. It was easy to keep his own counsel under the circumstances.

Woodcock drank as Askham watched him. He didn't even try to join him at the sideboard. He seemed to itch to leave. Crispin expected it when he said, 'Then we can leave this for the coroner as well.'

'I will await him,' said Crispin helpfully. The more helpful he was the sooner they would leave.

'That's right, you will,' said Woodcock, jabbing a finger at him as he swigged down the wine from the cup. He slammed the cup down on the sideboard and smoothed his mustache. 'Right, then. We'll be off. Do your work, Guest, and you won't run into any difficulties with the Lord Sheriffs' office.'

Crispin bowed, relieved as they made their way from the room. He listened as their mutterings and footsteps took them across the foyer and out the door.

'Thank God for that.' He sighed.

Nigellus and Rykener arrived in the parlor with a small chest. 'There's little space in my lodgings at Gray's Inn,' said Nigellus, staring forlornly at the pitiful coffer.

'Pray God it won't discommode you for long, Master Cobmartin. And . . . Eleanor.'

'But how will I change at your lodgings if you are bringing the cook?' asked John quietly, looking over his shoulder.

'I'll have him come after,' said Crispin. 'In fact, you should go now.'

'But . . .' Nigellus gestured upward toward the construction noise. 'I've told no one . . .'

'And you need tell no one where you are going. I'll convey it to the steward that all messages to you should come through me.'

'Dear me. Ordinarily I'd have William run back and tell them. Now . . .' He wiped at his eyes. 'Oh dear, oh dear.'

John was beside him in an instant, patting his shoulder.

'Jack, take them quickly.'

'Yes, sir. Come along, Master Nigellus. Hasten, now.'

Christopher joined them and Crispin watched them go, as strange a couple as he had ever known. But he couldn't help but like the two of them. He turned and headed for the steward's chamber. When he poked his head inside the door sitting ajar, he wasn't there. *Must be with the workmen*, he speculated. Up the stairs he went. The dust, the noise, all hung in the air on the first floor of the manor house. Men carrying lengths of wooden planks, plasterers with their buckets and spattered aprons, and all manner of apprentices carrying whatever their masters instructed them to. With so many, he wondered why it wasn't all complete already. Delays with the coroner visits no doubt cut into their time. For who did not wish to stop their work to watch the carrying of a dead body?

He searched amid the plaster dust lingering in the air for the figure of Philip Able. When he found him, he waited patiently as the steward directed the workmen to finish as quickly as possible. When the man turned at last, he nearly ran into Crispin.

'Oh! Master Guest. I thought you'd gone.'

'And just returned. I will await the coroner, but I wanted to inform you that Master and Madam Cobmartin will be . . . in another location for the moment. Should you wish to communicate with them, you may contact me on the Shambles.'

'And why is that? Where are they going?'

'They are leaving for their safety. I know where they will be lodged and I can get a message to them. And, indeed, Master Robert the cook will also be relocated. Again, for his safety.'

'The cook? What in heaven is happening here? We'll have no cook?'

'I daresay, you shall have to learn to fend for yourselves.'

'But this was supposed to be the most respected of houses. Why, you could ask anyone and they would say that the Cobmartin household was as wholesome as they came.'

'Murder does change things, Master Able.'

'But . . .'

'I have informed you. I will await the coroner below.'

He left the man to work it out and descended the stairs. The coroner arrived an hour later and after he and his men took away the body of William Roke, Crispin crossed himself and sought out the kitchens.

Robert was scrambling about as Crispin had seen before, stirring one pot, then tasting another, and all the while ordering his scullion to various tasks.

'Master Robert!' shouted Crispin above the din of clashing pots and crockery.

The cook glanced over his shoulder and frowned upon seeing Crispin. 'Master Guest, I am much too busy to talk to you now.'

'I'm afraid all will have to wait, good sir.'

'Eh?' He grabbed a cooking pot off the fire with the hem of his apron, and spun with it toward an already cluttered work-table. 'What's that you said?'

'You may put all that aside and come with me.'

He stopped, spoon midway to his lips. 'Put it aside? But dinner? It's nearly ready.'

'Your scullion will have to take care of that, Master Robert. Your masters have already left the house and they have ordered that you must go too.'

'Go? Go where?'

'I'm afraid to *my* household. It is . . .' Crispin lifted his eyes to the vaulted ceiling, '. . . a poorer place than this one. But there will be children to feed and such. It is for your safety, sir. Because of William Roke's murder.'

'William murdered?'

'Didn't you know?'

The cook eased himself to a stool, still clutching the tasting spoon. 'Maybe I heard something of it but I was so busy . . .' He belatedly crossed himself. 'And . . . why must *I* go?'

'Because I fear this death is related to Wilfrid Roke's death, and that the killer is still among you. And those who knew of Wilfrid in memory are in danger themselves.'

'God's toes. It's me and the master. We're the last to know.'

'Yes. And in danger. So you must come with me now.'

He looked to his pottage, to the other pots on the fire. 'And all this . . .'

'Here!' called Crispin to the scullion stoking the fire and clearing up the vegetable debris into a basket for the chickens. He looked up to Crispin with a sooty face. Crispin recalled him from the list as Roger. 'You must serve the dinner. And the rest of the meals for a while. Can you do that?'

He looked horrified, and he turned his face toward the cook. 'Master,' said the ruffled boy with hair like a hedgehog, sticking in all directions. 'I never done it on me own.'

'You'll do fine, Roger. Just . . . just make pottage. There's a good boy.'

'Just pottage?'

'You've seen me do it often enough. You can do it.'

'Aye, sir.' He glanced forlornly about the kitchen.

'Come now,' said Crispin. 'Have you things to pack?'

Crispin waited at the entrance for the cook to collect his clothing. He finally came with a cloak and traveling hat. He clutched a bag under his arm and blinked profusely. 'I've never left this house once since coming here as a boy. Not once.'

'The Cobmartins are very grateful for your faithfulness, sir. But we must be off.'

They set out onto St Martin's and headed left onto the Shambles.

'This is dreadful,' the man muttered, darting suspicious glances to the people on the street, from the boy with the spotted hog to the man carrying bundled fuel on his shoulders. 'How can it be that someone in our household could be a killer? We know everyone. And, as you say, only Master Cobmartin and me are remaining from those days. Who could it be?'

'I haven't worked that out yet, sir.'

'Where are we going? It looks like we're here on the Shambles.'

'We are, Master Robert, for that is where *I* live.'

'On the Shambles? How absurd.'

It was long past the time Crispin took umbrage at where his lodgings were located. 'It might interest you to know, Master Robert, that I think I have the name of the man that so peaked Madam Roke's interest. Was it not Thomas Courtney?'

'Yes! Yes, that's right. Thomas Courtney. My word. It's been years and a day that I've heard that name. Courtney it was. Have you found him?'

'I have yet to search for him, but I shall be at it very soon. Ah. Here we are.'

The old poulterer's stood on a corner. It had a ground and a first floor and a back garden big enough to accommodate two horses, several chickens, and a goat. Barely. Crispin had never lived in such close quarters with animals before. Not since his days in the army with Lancaster, but he was pleased that Jack's wife Isabel had been so enterprising. For now they had fresh eggs and milk when they needed it, which was more than he and Jack had ever had on their own, for Crispin hadn't known the first thing about caring for animals. They ate better these days, that was a certainty.

'We haven't much to our pantry, I'm afraid, Master Robert, but we make due. Eggs, goat's milk and cheese, and bread from the baker. There is meat but it is spare.'

'And you have a cook now?'

'My apprentice's wife. I'm certain you'll get along.'

Robert's skeptical expression seemed almost comical. As Crispin opened the door and announced to the house that he was home, three children came running. Little Crispin grabbed him by the waist, Helen by the leg, and Gilbert by his ankle. He laughed as he dragged them all forward. 'You little mongrels. Let go of me!' But he didn't say it harshly. He managed to get himself to a chair, sat, and peeled them off. He gathered them in his arms and kissed the tops of their ginger-haired heads. 'What mischief have you all got up to?'

They all chattered at once. Gilbert pointed his wet finger at Little Crispin, and Helen got her face into a frown and shook her head wildly, while Little Crispin sat stoically at all the accusations.

'It sounds like a lot of mischief to me,' said Crispin. 'But I have a visitor, so it's best you all go off on your own. Go to the back garden. Go!'

'But mummy says we mustn't, that we're under her feet,' said Helen. 'She's hanging laundry and Gilbert keeps putting his muddy hands on it.'

'Do not,' he said, holding up his muddy hands to show Crispin. 'They aren't muddy.'

Edging back, Crispin looked down at his stockings. Muddy handprints. 'Nevertheless, you must go. Fetch your mother.'

Helen, the little mother herself, grabbed hold of both her brothers – younger and older – and dragged them with her to the open back door. 'MOTH-ER!' she cried.

Robert chuckled. 'A full household indeed!'

'They are quite untamed, but they are good little imps.'

'They do you proud.'

'Alas, they are not mine. But my apprentice's.'

Robert gave him a studied look.

Crispin settled in his chair while Robert stood by as they both awaited the arrival of Isabel Tucker.

When she bustled in with children all about her exclaiming that Master Crispin brought a stranger, she shushed them and admonished them to go outside . . . which none of them did.

'Master Crispin, you've returned,' was all she said, giving him a nod and Robert a long scrutiny. Baby Genevieve was fast asleep and strapped to her back in a cobbled sling.

'Yes,' he said, scraping the mud from his left stocking with his right foot. 'Has Jack been here with Master and, er, Madam Cobmartin?'

Her gaze flicked again to Robert as she nodded. 'Aye, they'd come and gone with Christopher, nary a word of explanation.'

'I'm sure Jack will explain it when he returns. Later. Isabel, this is Robert, the Cobmartin cook. Master Robert, this is Madam Tucker. She rules the household with an iron hand.'

She gave Crispin a withering look. 'That is how you characterize it, then? Look at these creatures whom I told to go outside. Do they obey me?'

She swept her arm to show the three children, who were all looking up expectantly and quite innocently, much like three muddy cherubs.

'Don't let her fool you, Master Robert. In any case, Robert will be with us for a while. If he would be so kind as to cook for us, that is one less task you must perform, Isabel.'

'*Cook* for us?' Her eyes narrowed just that much.

'Yes. I understand that he is excellent at his task.'

Robert beamed at the praise and in the next breath began his assessment of the house. 'And the kitchens are outside?' he asked Isabel.

She folded her arms and gestured with her head. 'There lies the kitchen. This is no manor house, but a humble dwelling. The hearthfire is good enough for the likes of us.'

Robert snapped a furtive glance at Crispin, but he noted that the master of the house didn't flinch at the suggestion. Crispin had long ago lost the notion that he was more deserving of something better.

'Well then . . .' He looked around. 'Your pantry, madam? What haunches of meat have you? Your spices? May I assume you have on hand powder douce, powder fort, and white powder?'

Isabel squirmed, and hid it by adjusting the strap on her shoulder. 'This is a *humble* house,' she reminded him again. 'We haven't the extravagant spices that a larger house would have.'

'Dear me. This is unheard of. How can I be expected to provide the meanest of meals without suitable spices?'

'Er . . .' Crispin rose and stuffed his hand into his money pouch. 'Perhaps, Master Robert, after Isabel has shown you our supplies, you can purchase the rest of what we might need. Or, erm, at least some of them.' He left several coins on the table, tabulating in his head what he could afford to spend. With a last glance at Robert's despairing expression, he laid one more coin atop the others. 'I must be at my task. Good luck to you both.'

Out the door and on the street, Crispin took a deep breath. He had to get to Friday Street and see if he could find hide or hair of Thomas Courtney.

TEN

Friday Street was just off West Cheap. Crispin walked the lane, its shops and houses the same as the rest of London, though it was the tanners' street and smelled of it. Was it worse than the Shambles and the constant smell of offal and blood? Perhaps he had accustomed himself to the Shambles, for he did not smell it like he used to. But tanners . . . 'God bless them,' he muttered, adjusting the leather cape and hood sitting on his shoulders. The good leather of his hood had managed to survive the twenty-one years of his banishment. He couldn't help but reach up and smooth the crenellated hem of the soft leather between his fingers. Even now it kept the misty rain from his head.

He leaned into an open shop window where the shopkeeper and his apprentice were working over a piece of tanned leather of the trade and marking with chalk the various scars left behind on the hide. 'I beg your mercy,' said Crispin. The hide worker with a hawk-like nose looked up sharply. When he saw Crispin's demeanor and clothing, he straightened and bowed.

'Good sir,' he said, with a foreign accent, possibly from Flanders. 'How can I help you?' He still held the piece of chalk over the vaguely cow-shaped skin while his apprentice clutched the hide, holding it taut.

'I am looking for a family – and in all truth, I do not know if any remain on this street – by the name of Courtney.'

'Oh, indeed, they do reside here. You have only to pass down three more houses on this side of the lane to find them.'

'I am much obliged.'

Before he turned to go, the shopkeeper called out, 'Good sir, if I may ask, where did you acquire your fine capelet?'

'Dear me,' said Crispin, thinking. 'It was many years ago, sir. But it was London-made.'

The man smiled and nodded in acknowledgment. If it had

not come from this man then perhaps it was from one of his neighbors. Crispin bowed and left.

He counted down the doorsteps, and found himself before a tall, thin structure, wedged between a leather-worker's shop and a glover's. It had two stories above the ground floor, though the topmost was little better than a garret.

He stepped up smartly to the door and knocked. The door opened and an old man with white whiskers and wearing a long, dark blue gown shuffled to the threshold and looked Crispin over. 'Can I assist you?'

'You can. Is your name Courtney?'

'Yes, and the last of them stands before you.'

'Oh? I am looking for *Thomas* Courtney. I was told that he might have been a stonemason some twenty years ago.'

The man stroked his beard. His clothes were fine, if not a little worn. But Crispin had observed that some older men whose sight wasn't as good as it used to be often didn't take good care of their appearance. He wore few ornaments. He had a brooch at the shoulder and a necklace partially hidden by his beard.

'Thomas Courtney there was, and stonemason he was as well, going against the advice of his father, myself,' he said, laying a hand to his breast, 'but that Thomas Courtney went to his task one day and left his home and his father without word. It was very like him.' The last was said with some measure of distaste.

'Indeed. And when, may I ask, was this?'

'And who are you, good sir, that you should ask so many questions of a pain that still stabs at an old man's heart from so long ago?'

'Forgive me, Master Courtney,' he said with a bow. 'I am Crispin Guest. I am called the Tracker of London.'

'Tracker, eh? It seems I have heard of a man such as you. Do you track him now, when he is twenty years gone? Or do you bring dread tidings to me?'

'I do not, Master Courtney. I am merely looking for him. He might have been a witness to a dangerous misadventure some twenty years ago.'

'Dangerous misadventure. Well, that certainly sounds like

Thomas.' He looked Crispin over for another moment before shuffling back inside and beckoning to him. 'You might as well enter, Master Guest, and come out of the rain.'

Crispin glanced back to the street, where the gentle sprinkling had turned to a heavier veil of rain. He followed the man in and closed the door behind him. They retreated into a smaller chamber, warm and homey, with a servant tending to the fire. Courtney gestured to a second chair before the hearth while he lowered himself with grunts and creaking bones into the other. 'Ah!' he said, and settled in. 'London weather has crept into my bones at last. I used to wonder at the groans and moans of my grandfather when he moved from spot to spot and finally landed in his chair. I wonder no more. What can I tell you, Master Guest? Amery, get our visitor some wine.'

'Don't bother yourself or your servants, sir.'

'Well, *I* would like one. Do not let me drink alone.'

'Very well, then.'

'It is warmed on the fire. It helps thaw these old bones of mine.'

And mine too, thought Crispin. For though he was not as old as the man before him, his life had been hard these last two decades, and he felt just how hard it had been in his joints, when the weather was coldest.

The servant took Crispin's wet cloak and hood, and served him first, ladling the wine from the pot on the hearth, and then served his master. Crispin decided it was good that the man insisted. Not only was the wine in the cup warming his hand but also his chest as it went down. It was simmering with cloves, cinnamon, and other spices, and put his disposition into a congenial mood.

When Courtney had drunk a little, Crispin leaned forward in his seat. 'I take it your son, Thomas, had his own adventures.'

'Indeed he did. He was a handsome boy, you see. And . . . well. He found his pleasure in women. I fear he little abided whether they were married or not.'

'He was a stonemason?' Crispin looked around to see if he could spy any sign of such activity.

'He was. I was not. If you are wondering why a child of a

leather worker should choose to become a stonemason, look no further than the stonemason's daughter. He had an eye for her, and for her father's wealth.'

'Most unusual. Were you not as accomplished?' Crispin noted the tapestries, plate, and other finery on display, as well as the thick, carved furniture.

'Not as my son would have it. He seemed to enjoy the labor . . . and the fine figure it produced in him. Why a man would choose such harsh work to the careful indoor work of a leather worker . . .' He raised his hand in futility and let it fall to his thigh. 'Well, there it was. And with his comely figure he seemed to gather more beauties to him. He paid little heed to the stonemason's daughter after he'd become a master himself.'

'It seems very odd indeed. But I had heard somewhat of his . . . er, interests in women.'

'And all for naught. I wish I knew what became of him, where he lives now.'

'When he last left you, was it in distress, after an argument, perhaps?'

'Nothing but arguments. Several years before, he had obtained a "fat job" – this is what *he* called it – at a wealthy mercer's home. He confided that there was a woman he had fallen in love with there and had planned to run away with her. And so we argued. Mostly about his morality and equally about funds, for he begged me for the money to make a new life for himself and this woman.'

'Did he name the woman?'

He leaned back in his chair, idly stroking his beard with one hand, and clutching the necklace pendant with the other. 'It was so long ago.'

'If you can try . . .'

'I think it was . . .' He stopped stroking the beard to idly reach for the wine goblet. He tilted it to his lips and drank, eyes closing over the brim. 'Margaret, it might have been.'

And Margaret Roke was the woman who fell down the stairs not long before Wilfrid Roke went missing. Perhaps in his anger at Roke killing his lover, Thomas Courtney had decided to wreak vengeance upon Wilfrid, and murdered Wilfrid in that callous manner, then escaped to God-knew-where.

'I see,' was all he said aloud. 'How old was your son at that time?'

'Five and twenty. He'd be forty-five now. I've no inkling if I'm a grandfather or not.'

'And you have no idea where your son now resides? If he even resides in London.'

'I don't know. The amount of money he wanted, I assumed he would have left London, but since he didn't get it from me, I don't see how he could have afforded it. He'd likely still be in the city, unless his paramour had the funds.'

'And he hasn't contacted you in all this time?'

'Alas, no, he has not. I would have told him . . . well. I would have told him it was a foolish quarrel. I would have forgiven him.'

Crispin sipped his wine. It grew cold quickly out of the fire. 'Had you never searched for him?'

'A little. It was a rudimentary search, but nothing came of it.' He rubbed the pendant that turned out to be a cross once it peeked out of the man's beard. A small black stone was set in the middle of it.

'Had you contacted the stonemason's guild?'

'No. I suppose I should have gone there first.'

Crispin set his wine aside and stood. 'Then that is where I must go. If I find word of him, I will report back to you.'

'I would be most grateful, sir. Do you accept a fee? I should pay you for your services.'

'There's no need. I am already in service to another . . .'

'No, I wish to pay you. Every man must make his wage, and no doubt, you will earn yours.' He reached into a pouch at his belt and pulled out several silver coins. 'Will that suffice, Master Guest?'

'It is more than generous.' He took the thruppence and dropped it into his own pouch. 'Thank you, sir. God be with you.'

'And with you, Master Guest. May the Lord speed you in your quest.'

The servant helped Crispin on with his cloak and capelet. Crispin left the old man a little more than annoyed with the vain Thomas Courtney, who had left his father with no word of his location. And all for a woman. Crispin thought of his own long-ago adventures and how each one seemed to involve a woman. But instead of scowling at that past, he allowed himself to reminisce . . . and smiled.

His smile faded when he realized Thomas Courtney was likely a murderer. How was he to tell the old man that?

He set out for the stonemason's guildhall on Lime Street at the other end of town near the Tower. He supposed they kept records. Most guilds, lawyers, and clerks kept records from decades, even generations ago. It was one of the things Englishmen were good at – their record-keeping.

He ducked down a close to circumvent the main road, and as the shadows closed over him, he *almost* looked back at what he thought was the sound of a step behind him.

When the cudgel came down on the back of his head, he vaguely admonished himself for not taking better care.

His sight dimmed, and he stumbled to the ground in short order.

ELEVEN

He hadn't been knocked out completely, and from his place on his back on the damp cobbles, Crispin looked up into a blurry face bending over him. 'Not dead,' said the voice, mildly disappointed. He watched helplessly as the man raised his cudgel again to finish the job, when someone at the mouth of the close called out. The man looked sharply in that direction, lowered his avenging arm, and sprinted away, cloak covering the rest of him in a sweeping arc.

Two men rushed to his side, kneeling on the stones. 'Sir! Sir, are you all right?' they asked.

Crispin groaned, reaching slowly for the tender spot at the back of his head. It was damp with blood. He muttered a nonsensical acknowledgment that seemed to wash worry across their brows.

'Help me get him up,' said one of the men to the other.

Crispin wanted nothing more than to lie on the ground, but two sets of strong arms levered him upward and he leaned heavily on them, feet touching the ground at last, though he could barely feel them. When he could finally get his weight over his wobbly thighs – stomping his feet a few times to get the feeling back into them – he shakily let go of his rescuers. 'I . . . I thank you for your timely arrival.' He leaned a little too far to compensate and threw himself off balance. The man to his left grabbed his arm again until he could keep himself upright.

'Who was that?' asked the man on his right, a large man with ham-like arms and a prickle of ginger hair on his pate. 'Did he rob you?'

Crispin's hand snaked toward his money pouch, still at his belt. 'No. Did either of you see his face?'

The man on his left – a rangy man with a mop of dark hair and a frazzled beard – shook his head. 'It was too shadowed. And he ran like the devil was after him.'

'A shame.'

'You have many enemies?' asked the burly man on his right.

'Too many to count, I'm afraid.'

He caught the men exchanging glances.

'I would pay you for your gallant intervention,' said Crispin, reaching for his pouch.

The man on his left put his large hand over his. 'There's no need for that, friend. We did our Christian duty. Didn't we?' He raised a brow to the other man.

The burly man looked for a moment as if he'd disagree, but in the end he shrugged. 'I hope a stranger would come to my aid in similar straits, like the Good Samaritan.'

'Then you are blessed, indeed. I will mention you both in my prayers.'

The rangy man seemed ready to catch Crispin. 'Can we escort you home? Call on someone to attend to you?'

'No, thank you. I can make it on my own.'

He shook both their hands and after making certain one last time that Crispin was well enough, they escorted him through the close and left him to his own devices.

Crispin shouldered the wall, leaning heavily against it. His head was still swimming and he didn't trust that he could stand for long without puking. Who the hell was that attacking him? Did he recognize that voice? It was hard to remember. And as he had said to his own Good Samaritans, it could have been anyone. A disgruntled thief he had put before the sheriffs; a man he'd got into a brawl with over mistreatment of a servant . . . Anyone.

But he wondered if it had aught to do with his current investigation into Thomas Courtney. Or Thomas Courtney himself. Had *he* found Crispin? After all, he was likely at the Cobmartin house as a stonemason, though he hadn't gone by that name. And he could have overheard Crispin's thoughts on the matter. If he'd been following him . . .

He cast a glance over his shoulder. Sloppy to have been so overpowered. His senses weren't as acute as they used to be. This game was for a younger man. A man like Jack Tucker.

He should let Jack do more of the legwork. But he dreaded the idea of easing off. It meant that slow, downhill trek to becoming an old man. And though every knight feared it, he feared it more as a poor man than he ever would have as a lord. Or so he supposed.

Still, his head pounding with pain, he wasn't certain he had many years left as a Tracker. He didn't think his head could take it.

He took a deep breath and pushed himself away from the wall, seeing speckles of stars as he did. He breathed deeply again until the stars dispersed and he could stand on his own without fear of falling over or getting sick. It took a few moments. More than a few. He reached up and gently touched the spot. There was still blood on his fingertips but he didn't reckon there was much he could do about it.

Where had he been heading? Oh yes. The Mason's Guildhall, just down Lime Street. He took yet another deep breath and set out, a little wobbly still, but kept walking. At least the rain had stopped, leaving a mist hanging like a tattered veil down the soggy streets.

The guildhall was a magnificent structure using all the stone-masons' art, with several towers, crenellations and arches.

He knocked and a clerk answered the door. When Crispin

explained what he wanted, he was led to a small room where another clerk greeted him. 'I understand that you wish to locate a man, one of our guild?'

'Yes. I hope that you keep records of your members, for he was part of your proud guild some twenty years ago. I am seeking him wherever he may live, if still in London.'

'We all pay tithes to the guild to keep it strong and relevant. If he is still in London and a man of honor, he will have paid. What is his name?'

'Thomas Courtney.'

The man turned to the floor-to-ceiling shelves brimming with scrolls with long tags of leather. Ironically, these were tags Thomas Courtney could have supplied had he stayed a leather worker.

The clerk ran his hand along the many scrolls, stopping to pull one out occasionally to read the writing on the edge of the parchment, before shaking his head and tucking it back into place. It was very much like the steward's room back at the Cobmartin household.

Finally, he pulled a thick roll down, pinned the top edge to the top of his table, and began to unwind it, using his finger to scan down the page. 'I do not see this name on this year's tithe, Master Guest.'

'What of last year?'

The man carefully rolled up the sewn scroll, and placed it where he had pulled it from the shelf. His finger scanned again, and pulled another scroll. He did the same and unrolled it, and shook his head. 'Not here, either.'

Crispin stepped away, rubbing his chin. 'Can you check for twenty years ago?'

The man shrugged. 'Certainly.' He walked back and knelt at a low shelf, pulling out the sewn scroll. He unrolled it and ran his finger down the long list of names. 'Ah. Here he is.'

Crispin drew closer, eyes tracking over the many names. 'And does it mention his address?'

'It does. On Friday Street.'

'Go to the next year.'

The man sighed and without replacing the scroll, got the next year's. He could not find the name there.

'And so,' said Crispin, thinking, 'he did not tithe.'

'It appears he did not.'

'I don't suppose guild members are required to report whether they leave the city?'

'Not required, no. But it is a courtesy in order to join a different city's guild.'

'And this was not done?'

He rummaged around further among the scrolls, glancing at one and another. 'It does not appear to be so.'

'What would be the cause of such a thing?'

The clerk slowly rolled up the scrolls on his desk. 'Well, he couldn't work in the city without belonging to the guild. So he could be taking jobs illegally. That is certainly a possibility, but rare. He might have left the city in a hurry, or stopped work as a stonemason, or . . .'

'Or?'

'He died.'

'Or . . . he changed his identity.'

The clerk tucked the scrolls away. 'And why should he have done that?'

'In order to kill.' But twenty years ago, he hid himself. Twenty years. Lying in wait all this time, waiting to kill at the Cobmartins? Unlikely. 'It makes no sense.'

'Does it not?' the clerk said absently, adjusting scrolls.

'No, it doesn't. Well, thank you. I appreciate your time.'

'No doubt,' muttered the clerk. 'Oh. Sir, there is blood on your shoulder.'

Crispin turned to look at his leather shoulder cape. 'Yes. It is from an accident earlier.'

'God have mercy. Do you need aid, sir? It looks to be serious.'

'No. I will be fine.'

'But . . . but sir!'

'Thank you.'

Crispin left the guildhall and stood in the street, scouting the courtyard and the streets beyond. If the workmen belonged to one guild or another, then someone would have hired them for the Cobmartin household. He had to ask again at the house to discover who hired them and go over their names again. Perhaps one had gone missing today and been up to mischief, coshing Crispin on the head!

He was close to a solution; he could feel it. And yet, he didn't seem to have any idea what that solution was. Something teased at his memory, but he couldn't quite put his finger on it.

And yet, even if Thomas Courtney was the killer, why kill poor, innocent *William* Roke?

The streets seemed to be deserted as the bells rang Vespers. He hadn't realized it was so late. But as he ventured over the darkening streets, he felt a chill run up his spine. For was there not someone still stalking him? He couldn't stop glancing over his shoulder and it was not a good feeling. Never before had he feared strangers or threats. Maybe he *was* getting too old for this. His head still ached, and he noted more blood on his shoulder cape. He pulled the hood up over his head to stop the flow from showing.

He came to St Martin's Lane and the Cobmartin house. The lights from the glass-paned windows shone on the streets. Men standing around braziers, warming themselves, paid him little heed as he moved toward the gatehouse, where no one awaited him. He walked toward the front entrance and knocked, waited, knocked again. Finally, when he felt he'd waited long enough, he tried the door. It was open.

He strode across the entry and up the stairs unmolested, where the workmen were still at their labors by flickering lamplight, though it looked to Crispin that they were packing away their tools. They had enclosed the place where the dead man was found. Smooth plaster replaced the makeshift tomb, and other holes and doorways had been repaired and built as if they had always been that way. 'You men,' said Crispin aloud. Some looked up from tucking their tools in leather satchels. 'Have your complement of men been here all day?'

A workman with a smear of plaster on his cheek, blinked up at him as he wiped down his various trowels with a wet rag, scraping some of the crusty tools with a knife. 'All of us were here all the day. Where is Master Cobmartin? He usually bids us farewell for the night.'

'He is not here. I speak for him. Is all your number here now?'

The plasterer looked about. 'Aye. It looks to be all of us. Four men. And as many carpenters. They left earlier.'

'And what of a stonemason?'

'For three days, but he was done since yesterday. He finished the hearth in the room we just plastered.'

'He finished yesterday?'

'Aye. He was an older man, like you.'

'What was his name?'

'John Harrow.'

Crispin ran through the faces of the men he'd talked to that morning but didn't recall him. 'Did he mention having worked in this house before? Perhaps years ago?'

'He never said a word,' said the plasterer. 'Just worked on his own, laying stone after stone. He and his assistant.'

'And what was his assistant's name?'

'Tim somebody,' said another plasterer, gripping his satchel in his hand. 'A young man. An apprentice, likely.'

'Do either of you know where this John Harrow lives?'

The man with the satchel shook his head, but the other shrugged as he scrubbed the plaster from his cheek. 'I think it was Lime Street.'

Crispin turned to look out of the window. It was too late to knock on doors now. Best to get home. The thought of it called loudly to him, to be home and safe and in the comfort of his own hearth again. And maybe have Jack or Isabel see to his head.

'Very well. Good night to you. The steward is in charge. He will see to you if you have questions.'

'We're almost done. Another day or two at most,' said the man with the satchel. 'A good job, this was. Except for the, er, man in the wall.'

'Aye,' said the other with a shiver. 'A dead man is not good luck.'

'No, indeed,' muttered Crispin as he turned and left them, trotted down the stairs, and caught himself on the wall at the last moment when he stumbled. He desperately needed to get home and attended to. He felt weak and tired.

When he got to the street he hurried along to the Shambles, encountering no one on the darkening streets.

He reached his door at last, feeling an immense sense of relief when he pushed it open.

But instead of the calm and rest he expected – *hoped* for! – Isabel and Master Robert were at it hammer and tongs.

TWELVE

'You're using all our spices!' yelled Isabel. Her eyes were wide and wild and there was flour on her face and on her clothing. She hadn't noticed Crispin enter as she clutched several small ceramic pots to her chest like a babe, juggling them, trying to hold their wooden covers in place with her red, chapped fingers.

Robert, hair flailing in all directions and apron stained and askew, threw his hands up. 'How else can I make this meal fit for consumption?'

Whatever was in the pot on the hearth smelled good enough to Crispin. He hadn't realized how hungry he was.

Isabel settled the pots on the table and stood protectively in front of them. 'Every meal *I* make in this house,' she said precisely and in a deadly voice that Robert hadn't the familiarity to recognize, 'has *always* been fit to eat.'

'I don't see how,' said Robert.

'Master Robert,' said Crispin, jerking forward, slipping himself between them in hopes of stopping an imminent brawl. 'I think Madam Tucker's opinion must take precedent. After all, *she* is the, er, cook in this household.'

She nodded in satisfaction; chin raised.

'I thought I was to be brought here to cook.'

'You were brought here, Master Robert, to be safe. And I mistakenly thought that Isabel would appreciate the help.'

Isabel suddenly looked chastened. 'Oh, Master Crispin. I'm so sorry. Here you gone and done something nice for me. I'm not ungrateful, truly I'm not.'

'I failed to take into account how much you are used to running this household. I have not paid attention, and for that *I* am truly sorry. Forgive me, madam.'

'There's no need to apologize, Master Crispin . . .'

'Then what am I to do?' Robert, voice petulant, smoothed back his hair from his face.

'Enjoy a little respite.' Crispin didn't expect his vision to suddenly create two of each of them. 'And be grateful you—' He never got out the last words. Darkness closed in on his vision like a tunnel folding smaller and smaller, and the next thing he knew, he was falling . . . and then suddenly in his own bed with a concerned Jack and Isabel bending over him.

'What have you gone and done to your head, sir?' said Jack, tucking the bandaging around his scalp against his pillow.

Crispin wanted to sit up but thought better of it. He reached up and brushed Jack's hand away. 'I didn't do it to myself. I was ambushed.'

Jack expelled an exasperated sigh. 'What now?'

'I was hit on the head. The culprit had every intention of killing me . . . until he was interrupted.'

'I hope you left him with some bruises.'

'I'm afraid I didn't. He caught me unaware. From behind.'

'You are the most dangerous man in London. How the sarding hell did *he* get the better of *you*?'

'Jack!' hissed Isabel, pushing at his arm. 'Language!'

He ignored his wife and tilted toward Crispin. 'Well?'

Most dangerous man in London, he huffed. *Not for many a day.* 'I . . . wasn't paying attention,' answered Crispin aloud, angry suddenly.

'Christ!' Jack pushed up at his ginger curls and stomped away from the bed before circling back. 'You're my master. You've taught me everything I know. You should know better than to drop your guard.'

'I never expected that someone should be stalking me, Tucker! And keep your voice down. My head pounds like a bell.'

'Oh, master, I'm sorry. I am. Listen to me make it worse for you.'

Crispin reached up and found Jack's hand. 'You mean no harm. Indeed, it is good to be home and in your care. The both of you.' He lay back and closed his eyes. 'I'm not certain, but I think it has to do with the murders at the Cobmartins'.'

'God blind me,' muttered Jack, stroking his beard and sitting on the edge of Crispin's bed.

'He spoke to me,' Crispin continued. 'Well, he wondered why I wasn't dead yet.'

Jack leaned in eagerly. 'Did you recognize his voice?'

'I thought for a moment I had . . . but now it's gone.' He settled himself more comfortably on the pillow, and Jack leant a hand to help him.

'What did he look like, master?'

Crispin tried to recall, but it was no good. 'It was dark and my mind is blurry on it. No help there. But I went back to the house and I discovered that Wilfrid Roke's wife was carrying on with a stonemason, and through my investigations, I discovered who it was. But the stonemason working at the Cobmartin household does not go by that man's name. Yet . . . it could be him. We'll have to find the man and question him.'

'Or . . . maybe it's simpler,' said Jack. In a whisper he thumbed over his shoulder. 'What of Master Robert?'

'You mean you brought a murderer into my house?' hissed Isabel. 'Oh! The children!' She scrambled out of the room and thundered down the stairs.

Crispin gave his apprentice a withering look. 'There's no call to believe it is Robert.'

'But he was there at the time of the first crime.'

'But he could not have killed *William* Roke. He was in the kitchens. His scullion said so.'

'Do you trust his scullion to tell the truth?'

'You were once a scullion. Should I not trust you?'

Jack grumbled in reply.

'Tomorrow we will find this stonemason, John Harrow of Lime Street. He might just be Thomas Courtney, the man I was looking for.'

'That's for tomorrow,' said Jack, tucking the blankets around Crispin. 'You rest. I'll fetch you some food if you are able to eat it.'

'I'm starving. I will eat it even if I must lie flat to do so.'

'I'll help you, sir.'

Voices rose below. Isabel and Robert were at it again. Crispin moaned and he made to get up. Jack pointed a finger into his face and pushed at his shoulder. '*You* stay there. *I'll* see to it.' Jack pushed up his sleeves and stomped from the room, and soon a third voice was raised along with the others, but after the commanding tones of his apprentice had silenced the others,

Crispin sank back into his bed, at peace that Jack was taking care of it all.

As Crispin rose – gingerly – in the morning light, head still aching, but his double vision gone, he sighed in relief. He was to live yet another day. When Jack brought in his hot water for a shave, his apprentice offered to do it for him. Crispin thought that the wiser course.

As he sat in a chair in front of his chamber's hearth, warm cloth on his face, Jack talked and stropped the razor. 'Sir, it was kind of you to offer Master Robert to give my Isabel some relief, but I had no idea how . . . how . . . *invested* she was in her kitchen. I suppose a woman gets it into her head that the hearth is her domain, so to speak. And she fought as viciously as any chatelaine with a castle under siege. You should have seen her, sir.'

'Oh, I did.'

Tucker ticked his head as he smoothed the soap cake in his hands, lathering it, before he smeared it on to Crispin's stubbled face. He moved Crispin's face to one side to pull the razor over the beard on his chin. 'It's a shame it had to come to that. That woman works too hard, and with all them babes. She's a martyr, she is.'

Crispin smiled slightly, not wishing to give Tucker a chance to cut him.

'Why, I've never seen a woman more devoted to her household. We are both lucky to have her.'

Crispin acknowledged this with a sound in his throat.

Jack tilted up Crispin's chin and ran the razor up his neck. 'It's not that she's ungrateful, sir. Never that. Just . . . territorial. She'd never hurt you for the world.'

His throat having gone unslashed, Crispin relaxed as the razor moved expertly up his cheek.

'I have set Master Robert to tending to the children,' Jack continued. 'He objected at first, but they won him over. You should see him now, playing with them in the yard.'

The warm towel smoothed over his face, taking away the soap and small hairs. 'All's well that ends well, then,' said Crispin.

'It would seem so, sir. But it would be best to get this murder cleared up as soon as possible. That way Master Robert may return home.'

'I will see to it, Jack. With your help.'

Jack offered him hot porridge from the hob, and they both ate in Crispin's chamber. Jack helped him dress, and then they both set out – with an admonition from Jack to his family to behave themselves – into the chill morning.

The skin was still tender on the back of his head, so Crispin kept his hood up to protect it. He kept his guard up, too, even as Jack swiveled his head like a hawk searching for prey.

'I sent Master Walcote home,' said Jack. 'He will join us later if he is able, I suppose. But he does have more of a fitting vocation to attend to. It was . . . nice . . . him being with us. With you, sir.'

Crispin warmed at the thought, but then frowned. Yes, he enjoyed Christopher's company but the boy didn't belong with Crispin. It was better he stayed away. Though, if he had inherited Crispin's stubbornness – and there were all the signs that he had – he'd be back. The boy had all but promised him . . . even after Crispin's misstep with his mother.

They headed east and found the street they wanted off Fenchurch. Jack took the lead and marched up to the first shop they found.

'Good sir,' he asked of the merchant, 'know you of a John Harrow, stonemason?'

'Aye,' said the man with the shaggy beard and furred cloak. He jabbed his index finger up the street. 'He's in the shop up the street with the sign of the hammer and chisel.'

'Thank you, good sir. God's blessings.' Jack bowed and started up the street.

Crispin paused. 'Sir, do you know of anyone on this street by the name of Thomas Courtney?'

'Courtney, eh? Now let me think.' He scratched at his chin through his beard.

'He'd be a stonemason as well.'

After a moment or two, he shook his head. 'That name stirs no memories.'

'Then I thank you.' He gave the man a nod and hurried to catch up to Jack.

'What did you ask him, sir?'

'If he knew of Thomas Courtney. He did not.'

'You think he's John Harrow.'

'We will see.'

Ahead were similar signs hanging from stakes jutting out from over lintels, with trowels, hods, and hammers . . . until they saw the hammer and chisel.

Jack knocked upon the door and stood in front of Crispin protectively. When the door opened, a man in an apron looked them over before his eyes widened. He slammed the door in their faces.

Jack glanced once at Crispin before he shouldered the door open. They both saw the man retreat out the back door.

'Off you go, Jack,' said Crispin, feeling a bit old to be telling someone else to pursue their quarry, but there it was. He was too unsteady to go chasing all over London. As Jack flew out the back door, Crispin took a seat at the man's hearth – and a magnificent one it was – and settled in.

THIRTEEN

Jack followed the man over the wall of his garden, leaping up to grab the top of the wall and using the momentum to propel himself over. When he landed on the other side, he looked both ways and saw the tail-end of the man's apron fluttering behind him and disappearing around a corner. *Oh, no you don't*, thought Jack and sprinted after him.

He skidded around the corner, nearly upending an old woman carrying a meal sack on her head. He made his apologies with a bow, even as she harried him with language he couldn't believe an old woman knew, but he scrambled ahead leaving her behind, keeping his eye on Harrow.

The mason turned the corner again in front of Jack, and Jack pumped his arms and sped on, but when he turned that corner, he stumbled to a stop.

All around him was a site of new construction, with

scaffolding, cranes, and carts, and all manner of masons with the same kind of aprons milling and working. 'God blind me!' he swore. His eyes flicked from this man to that. Harrow had dusty blond hair cut to just below his ears and a beard. But they all had their backs to him. *A needle in a meadow!* he bemoaned.

He plunged in, grabbing likely candidates and whirling them about, much to their annoyance. He dodged one man taking a swing at him, and danced around another, enraged that Jack had made him drop his hod of bricks.

Jack thought all was lost, until something caught his attention out of the corner of his eye. The man seemed nervous, fidgety, and kept looking back at Jack. Finally, he couldn't seem to keep himself calm enough to hide among the many, and suddenly took off running. A blond man.

'Got you!'

Jack pushed himself away from the angry masons surrounding him with a mumbled apology, and set his feet to running hard over the cobblestone street. The man kept going, looking back with wide, anxious eyes, especially when Jack moved faster.

Jack smiled when Harrow turned into an alley, for Jack knew it was a dead end. He found Harrow at the wall, face awash in fear.

Jack pulled his dagger. 'And now, my man. It's time for you to face my master.'

'Please. I didn't mean to. I was coerced.'

'A dead man is still a dead man.' Jack closed on him and grabbed his arm in a tight grip. He kept his knife unsheathed and at the ready.

'A dead man?' cried Harrow. 'What are you talking about?'

'I'm talking about murder and the gallows. I think it's high time you were introduced to the latter.'

'No! Wait.' He dug in his heels and wriggled, trying to wrest his arm from Jack's unforgiving clasp.

'Steady,' said Jack, showing him the dagger blade. Harrow stopped struggling. 'I don't want to use this, Master Harrow, but I *will* do in the name of my master. Now come along.'

'But I didn't kill anyone,' he pleaded as Jack dragged him along. He pulled him down a different street than the construction and away from the disgruntled masons. Even though

passers-by looked at the two of them peculiarly, no one challenged them. Jack wondered if he were recognized as the
Tracker's apprentice. It gave him a spring in his step to think
about it.

'And isn't that what they all say.'

'All who say? I don't know what you mean and why you are
detaining me. Who are you?'

'I'm Jack Tucker, apprentice to Crispin Guest, the Tracker
of London.'

'The Tracker? Oh, no! Please! Don't take me to him. I didn't
do what you say I did.'

'Save it for my master.'

Jack hustled the man forward, sometimes dragging him,
sometimes pushing him on. Back to the man's shop where they
found Master Crispin sitting in a chair, cleaning his nails with
the sharp tip of his dagger.

The man resisted and Jack hooked his arm around Harrow's
neck and forced him into the chair opposite. 'He said he didn't
mean to do it, that someone coerced him.'

Master Crispin looked up mildly, lids low over his steely
gray eyes. 'Indeed. And who might that be, Master Harrow?'

'Your man said he thinks I killed someone. I didn't. I swear
by Almighty God.'

Master Crispin glanced up at Jack standing over the man
before he squared on Harrow again. 'Let me get this clear in
my mind. You say now that you didn't kill anyone. Then why
did you run?'

Harrow ran his hand over his face and beard. His cheeks and
forehead were swathed in perspiration. 'I . . . I recognized you
and your man. I . . . I stole from the Cobmartins. *I* didn't want
to. But one of the plasterers said he'd pay me for it if I took
it. I never would have. I never done anything like that before.'

'Stole what?' said Master Crispin.

The man wiped his face again. He said nothing but his eyes
darted to an ambry.

Master Crispin rose and strode to the cupboard and opened
the doors. There were assorted folded linens and blankets, and
atop them all, a silver candlestick. Master Crispin reached in
and clasped the candlestick and turned with it. 'This?'

Harrow dropped his head and nodded.

'And what else have you stolen, Harrow?' asked Master Crispin.

The man began blubbering and Jack smacked him on the side of his head. 'Answer him!'

'Nothing! On my oath, sir!'

'What do you know of these murders, then?'

'Nothing! God have mercy!'

Master Crispin glared. 'Did you ambush me yesterday on the street?'

Harrow's face projected puzzlement. 'No. Why would I do that?'

'Indeed. Why?' He folded his arms over his chest. 'Do you know a man, a mason, by the name of Thomas Courtney? Think carefully. I shouldn't want you to lie to me.'

Harrow pressed his hands together in prayer, folding his fingers over each hand. 'Courtney, Courtney . . .' he murmured. 'I . . . I . . .'

'Think carefully,' said Master Crispin.

'I am . . . thinking carefully. I, er, I do not know this man.'

'You are certain?'

'Yes. Yes.'

'Then . . . who was the man that bid you steal that item?'

'His name is Walter Perchay, my lord. He's one of them plasterers. The younger one.'

'And why didn't the miscreant merely steal it himself?'

Harrow licked his lips. 'Because I was the one in the room where the candlestick was.'

He snorted. 'I see.' Master Crispin sat for a moment longer with his eyes on Harrow – not moving, barely breathing – before he rose, set the candlestick on the table, and walked slowly toward Harrow squirming on his chair. He bent over and looked the man in the face, but Harrow turned his eyes away. Guest gripped his collar in his fist and yanked the man forward, leaving him at an awkward angle. He had no choice but to look at Master Crispin as he balanced on one knee, trying not to fall out of the chair completely. 'You're not masquerading as John Harrow, are you? You're not instead this Thomas Courtney?'

'No! I told you, I don't know the man.'

He squirmed in Master Crispin's grasp. 'I tell you what I am

going to do, Harrow. I will return this stolen item to the
Cobmartins, and if I find that you are lying to me . . . about
anything . . . I will return here and put the rope around your
neck myself.'

Harrow blubbered in reply.

'Consider yourself lucky that I don't wish to bother the
sheriffs with you.'

When Master Crispin let him go, Harrow did fall out of the
chair and onto his knees. He shuffled toward Master Crispin
and grabbed the hem of his crimson cote-hardie. 'Oh, thank
you, sir! Bless you, sir!'

Master Crispin bent over and tore the man's hands from his
coat. 'Behave yourself from now on, Harrow. I've got my eye
on you.'

He whimpered into his hands as Master Crispin signaled Jack
to pick up the candlestick. They left the man's lodgings and
shut the door after them.

'So you believe him, sir?'

Master Crispin shrugged. 'He was too frightened to lie to
me.'

'And what makes you think he *isn't* this Thomas Courtney?'

'Thomas Courtney has dark hair and is supposed to have a
beguiling face. That man has neither.'

Jack studied the candlestick as they walked. 'Is this Walter
Perchay a murderer?'

'I doubt it, but I shall have to question him.'

'I should make a stop to the Cobmartins today at Gray's Inn
to make certain they are faring well.'

'Good idea. Do so now. I'll take that.'

Jack handed the candlestick to Master Crispin. 'Are you
certain you don't need me, sir?'

'I'm not going to fall over, Jack.'

'Well, it's on your head if you do.'

Master Crispin whipped around to stare at Jack . . . and
cracked a smile.

FOURTEEN

Nigellus thought it was a very small lodgings before, but with the two of them crammed together in such a tight space, well . . . Still, they made the best of it, though Nigellus was itching to get back to his work . . . and to discover what was transpiring back at home.

'Oh, do sit down, Nigellus. You're like a nervous cat.'

He had been standing before the small hearth in his stocking feet, staring into the embers. 'I'm sorry, my love. I'm just worried.'

John shook his head and bent toward his embroidery beside a candle. At least *he* could get to *his* commissions, Nigellus thought with a sigh.

'You worry so much,' said John.

'That someone was trying to kill us? Yes, I do worry.'

John rested his small embroidery frame in his lap and looked up. 'If one of us must worry, I prefer to leave it to you.'

He cocked his head. 'Why?'

John smiled. 'You do it so well.'

He scoffed and turned back to the fire. The only thing good that could be said about this was that John could be in his men's clothing here and Nigellus did prefer it. But he knew well that it wouldn't take very long for John to become irritated and tire of their sequestration. He was a man who enjoyed his meals, his entertainments, his friends. Living as a monk was certainly not John's idea of paradise.

'I do wonder how Master Guest is getting along,' said Nigellus.

'Crispin is a clever man. He'll get the culprit.'

'Murder. On our grounds.'

'Not the first, though.'

Nigellus sighed. No, it certainly wasn't the first. He didn't see how they'd ever use those rooms. For guests, perhaps. Guests they didn't like.

A knock on the door froze them both. Nigellus looked at John and John motioned for him to answer.

Nigellus strode to the door and opened it only slightly. It was one of the pages from the school. 'Master Cobmartin?'

'Yes, boy?'

The page handed him a folded missive. 'For you, sir.' Nigellus turned it over in his hands and wandered back into the room.

John gave a disgusted huff and rose from his place. Digging into his money pouch, he gave the boy a coin, thanked him, and closed the door. 'You are so absent-minded at times,' he muttered and retrieved his embroidery.

Nigellus stood by the hearth and unfolded the parchment, that had neither wax seal nor ribbons. When he read it he gave out a squeak.

'What is it, Nigellus? A bill? We are always getting bills.'

'God have mercy.' He clutched the parchment to his chest.

'Well? What is it? 'Slud, Nigellus, you're as white as a winding sheet.'

But he couldn't. He couldn't read it aloud. With a shaking hand he held it toward John, who fairly snatched it from his hand.

'So what is this? *I know what you are,*' he read aloud. '*I know what sins the two of you get up to. Your father, rest his soul, would be ashamed if he knew. But if you don't want it known throughout London you will pay me the amount of thirty marks . . .* What the devil?' John looked up. 'We're being extorted? By God, I will slay the churl with my own dagger!'

'No, no! John, you mustn't make a fuss. Dear me, dear me.' His fingers teased at his lips and chin. He felt the scratch of stubble he had missed with his razor. 'I was afraid something like this would happen some day. But we've been so careful. My business. We'll be ruined! And I've so many bills to pay.'

John tossed his embroidery aside again, fisted the parchment in his hand, and jumped up to embrace his lover. 'Nigellus, sweeting,' he cooed to his temple, placing a soft kiss there. 'You must calm yourself. It isn't as if I have never been similarly extorted. It used to happen every other festival week. This is no different. We pay it, or I find the knave and beat him within an inch of his life. Or possibly both.'

Nigellus, though stricken, stared at John anew. 'You've . . . you've *beaten* a man?'

John tossed his long hair over his shoulder and raised his chin. 'Of course I have. I'm no weakling.'

'I know you're not. You're so much braver than I am.'

John brooded. 'I've had to be. You've been in your little world of courts and lawyers. You're like a chessman, my love. No one thinks about you other than your purpose. They don't dream you have a life, and loves, and cares, and joys.'

The stark words stabbed at something at his core. He felt a wash of heat over his cheeks. 'Thank you very much,' he muttered tightly.

'Oh love, *I've* never thought that. Just . . . people.'

'I never even thought about men this way until I met you.'

'My dear, naive Nigellus. You've been so busy being a lawyer, your nose in books. But you must remember; *I* was on the streets, plying my trade. I had to be open or I'd get no clients. And if I didn't fight back, they'd think they could beat *me*. *That*, I couldn't allow.'

'You *are* braver than I am.'

John's arms came around and embraced him again. 'I've always thought you were very brave and very clever. Reading all those books, memorizing the law, helping the innocent escape tragedy. If you weren't there, what would have happened to our friend Crispin?'

Yes, he was proud of that, though it was more the work of Jack Tucker that freed Master Guest from the gallows. Part of the work, he supposed.

He sagged in John's arms. 'What does it say we are to do?'

John lifted the parchment again and read: '. . . *you will pay the amount of thirty marks and leave it at the Standard cistern on Cheap at Sext on Thursday.*' He snorted. 'Doesn't even have the bollocks to face us. I'm going to spy on this lout and tell him what for.'

'We should just pay the money.'

'And have him come back to us as his own personal money pouch whenever he likes? I don't think so.'

'But, John . . .'

'You can't let people like that win, Nigellus. You, of all people, should know that. We'll trap him, I'll beat him, and leave him with a warning to leave us alone. It's a solid plan.'

'You're talking about committing an illegal act!'

'How can it be illegal when he is the one extorting *us*?'

Hands on his head in frustration, Nigellus sat on one of the chairs that didn't have piles of parchments on them. 'What are we going to do?'

Another knock on the door froze them again. But this time, John stomped to the door and cast it open, seemingly ready for full battle with the poor unfortunate . . .

Nigellus felt instant relief when he saw that it was Jack Tucker.

Before Jack could speak, John grabbed him by his collar and dragged him inside, shutting the door after him.

'What's amiss? Let go of me, Rykener!'

'This!' he said, waving the missive in Jack's face. 'This is amiss. Read it.'

'If you stop waving it in my face.' Jack snatched it as it went by again and flattened it. 'God's blood!' he cried.

'Indeed!' said John, flushed, pacing with very little space to do so.

'Where did you get this?'

Nigellus was biting his nails, a habit from childhood that he thought he'd left behind. He pulled his fingers from his mouth. 'Just now. A page brought it.'

'A page? Whose page?'

'From Gray's Inn. I know the lad.'

'But Nigellus,' said Jack, taking a moment to peer out the window. 'No one's supposed to know you're here. How did they send it here, then?'

John stopped his pacing and shot a worried look at Nigellus. 'Good God,' squeaked Nigellus. 'I hadn't even thought of that.'

'We've got to get you out of here,' said Jack, pulling out their chest from under the table.

John had the look of a stone gargoyle with mouth agape. 'Where will we go?'

Jack helped stuff the papers Nigellus tossed to him into the chest. 'I don't know. An inn, maybe? But we've got to leave here.'

'Wait,' said John. 'Should I . . . should I put my Eleanor clothes on?'

Jack looked him up and down, mouth twisting in thought. 'Aye. That would be better, I think.'

He scrambled for the chest, pushing the papers out of the way, and pulled out a long cote-hardie. He peeled off the coat he was wearing and tossed it toward Jack and pulled the dress over his head, furiously buttoning. 'My hair! Where is my veil?'

Nigellus stopped his own packing to help him.

Deftly, John plaited his hair into two braids, and wound them at his ears, pinning them on each side of his head. He took the veil Nigellus offered him and flew it over his head. With more pins stuffed between his lips, he used them to fasten the veil carefully and expertly into place.

'Do I look all right?' he asked, shooting a desperate expression toward Nigellus.

Nigellus took a moment to look at the man he loved. He smiled. 'You look lovely.'

It had taken John aback, but when he recovered, two ruddy blushes bloomed on his cheeks.

Jack lugged the chest with two hands. 'No dawdling. Are you ready?'

'Yes,' said Nigellus. They scrambled down the stairs and through the courtyard of Gray's Inn. Jack told them to wait at the edge of the courtyard while he talked to the porter at the gate. They waited until the page who had delivered the missive arrived.

Jack walked over to them and leaned over, a hand on the boy's shoulder. 'Now, m'lad,' he began, 'do you remember bringing a letter to Master Cobmartin?'

The boy turned to look at the tall woman, where women were not allowed. 'Aye. I did, not too long ago.'

'This is important, boy. Who gave you the missive?'

'He didn't say his name.'

'What did he look like?'

The boy rubbed his head in thought. 'Not as tall as you, sir. Maybe Master Cobmartin's height. Dark hair. Beard.'

'Well-spoken?'

'Not as good as Master Cobmartin.'

'And his age?'

'Older than Master Cobmartin.'

'How was he dressed?'

'Homespun. Not like a merchant or clerk. Like a workman.'

Jack gritted his teeth. Nigellus had the feeling that Jack might know who it was. 'Listen, lad, I will need you to come with us for only a bit. Your masters said it was all right. I want you to scout with me, looking around, to see if you can see the knave.'

'Was it a bad letter?' said the boy, suddenly upset.

Nigellus ruffled the boy's hair. 'You mustn't worry yourself over something you had no control over. We just need your help for now.'

That seemed to mollify the child, and he attended again to Jack Tucker. 'We'll just need you a little ways into London. All right?'

The boy nodded.

'Good lad. Let's go, then. And hasten.'

They set out. Jack kept his eyes peeled, looking over his shoulder, off to the side, ahead. Nigellus couldn't stop thinking that at any moment someone would shoot an arrow or come at them with a cudgel. The whole thing was damnable.

He cast a glance at John, dressed like a proper lady, and he didn't seem the least bit discomfited. No doubt his anger sustained him. And how *did* that miscreant find out where they had gone? Obviously, they had been following them. What a dreadful thing! For the rest of his life he'd never get over it, he was certain.

'Master Tucker!'

They stopped suddenly and, nervous, Nigellus looked to the man who called out . . . but it was only that Walcote boy. Nigellus didn't mind. Crispin Guest did have an unusual collection of followers. But Christopher – he thought his name was – seemed like a congenial lad. He'd helped them in their move to Gray's Inn, after all.

'What's going on? Good day, Master Cobmartin. Er . . . *Madam* Cobmartin.' He glanced at the page who was busy looking around. 'I thought you were to stay at Gray's Inn.'

'Dear boy,' said John with a smile.

Jack got in close to Christopher and said in hushed whispers, 'We are moving the Cobmartins from their seclusion to another hiding place, but I've run out of ideas.'

'Oh! They can come home with me.'

'Ah, now Christopher . . .'

'That sounds like a splendid idea!' chirped John.

'Ryk— Er, *madam*, I do *not* think it a good—'

'But there's plenty of room,' said Christopher. 'My father is on the road traveling. My mother would be fond of the company.'

Jack's face was stark and glazed as if in shock. But he looked toward Nigellus and John and seemed to give up. 'Aye, I suppose that will do. What will my master think of this?' he muttered. But he gave the page a coin, thanked him, and sent him on his way back to the lawyer's inn, admonishing the boy to keep quiet about it, and led the way of his company toward the Walcote residence.

Nigellus observed Mercery with a judicious eye. He had catered to many a merchant on the clothmonger's street and thought he knew which house it was they were heading for. He nodded to himself as they veered toward the large structure with its own fortress of a wall. They passed through the gatehouse with its porter who nodded to the lad, and straight up the stairs into the wide foyer, grander than his own. Though his father and brother were mercers, no one excelled like the Walcotes, and that was plain by every sight that assailed him: tapestries, servants in abundance, fresh flowers in a vase. He glanced toward John and worried that his paramour was looking around and getting ideas.

Christopher Walcote told a servant to fetch his mother, and then he invited them all to the parlor, where he himself offered refreshment. They declined, but sat or stood next to the large hearthfire.

Presently the door opened and Madam Walcote, a comely woman in her middle years, strode in. She had a cheery face but dreamy eyes, half-lidded, though she seemed to see all. Her hair was brassy gold and she looked about at her unusual guests with aplomb. And when she opened her mouth, Nigellus was surprised to hear the accent of a chambermaid.

'Christopher, what is this about? Greetings, Master Tucker.'

Jack bowed respectfully.

'Everyone,' said Christopher proudly, 'this is my mother,

Philippa Walcote. Mother, this is the lawyer I told you about, Master Nigellus Cobmartin. And this is Eleanor Cobmartin.'

She gave a curtsey to Nigellus and drew her brows in at meeting John, as some women were wont to do. Seldom did he fool the women.

'Eleanor, is it?' she said, somewhat skeptically.

'To my friends,' said John, raising his voice to a higher timbre.

'Well. Christopher's friends are always welcomed here—'

'Mother, I fear it is more than that. You see, these are Crispin's clients.'

At the mention of Master Guest, Madam Cobmartin's demeanor changed ever so slightly. Her eyes shone that much more, her face, already fresh with blooms of color on her cheeks, seemed to enliven. 'And what do they have to do with us?'

'Jack here says they are in trouble and in need of shelter. And I told them they could stay with us.'

She said nothing for a long beat, her mouth poised open in thought.

'Master Walcote,' said Nigellus, intervening into what was sure to be a long but polite refusal, 'I do not wish to inconvenience this household. Our troubles are not your troubles.'

Christopher waved his hand at Nigellus as if dismissing him. It reminded him of an opponent's dismissal in court some years ago, trying to lord it over Nigellus, the fresh-faced lawyer. If he rightly remembered, Nigellus had won that case. As he opened his mouth to object again, Christopher interrupted.

'Mother, they are very much in trouble. Do you remember when I told you about the house that had a skeleton in the wall? Well? That's their house!'

Poor Madam Walcote, thought Nigellus. *Her brows would never come down again.*

'And then there was another murder, so Crispin thought *they* would be next. The place they were hiding out was discovered and they need a better sanctuary. I shall make certain the porter is in the gatehouse and the footman guard the door. They'll be safe here . . . and they'll be company for you while Father is away.'

Something seemed to dawn on Madam Walcote's face and she turned to her son with a stern mouth. Nigellus wondered what it could be to cause such an expression, but clearly, Christopher was aware that she had worked it out.

'I-is that all right, Mother?'

Madam Walcote gusted a deep sigh and motioned toward Jack and the coffer he still held. 'You'd best set that down, Master Tucker. A servant will see to it to bring it to their chamber. Of course you are welcome here. Was, er, this by chance Master Guest's idea?'

'No, madam,' said Jack. 'I don't know what he'll say when I tell him.'

He had such a forlorn look on his face that even Madam Walcote had to chuckle. 'I see. Master Cobmartin, is it?' she said to Nigellus. 'Me husband used to speak very highly of your father and then your brother Augustus.'

'And Augustus always spoke well of Clarence Walcote. I believe he was at my brother's funeral.'

'I was sorry to hear of it. God have mercy.' She crossed herself. 'And now you reside there, at your father's house? But of course you do. Where were you before? You're a lawyer, I heard tell.'

'Oh, I lived here and there. I own a few properties in London. Master Guest's lodgings, for one. But it is nice to get back to my family home. Well . . . was. Before all the unpleasantness.'

She smiled indulgently. 'Let us get you situated.' She walked right up to John and hooked her arm with his. 'Eleanor, you must tell me how you met Crispin. I'm dying to hear your tale.' They walked together out of the parlor, giggling and whispering like two old friends.

Nigellus blinked at Jack.

'Well, Master Cobmartin, I will apprise my master of this new situation, and of the other with that letter. In fact, give it here so I can show him.'

Nigellus pulled it from his pouch and handed it over. 'I truly think that we should pay it.'

'Not on your life,' said Jack, tucking it into his own pouch. 'I will talk to Master Crispin. We might be here tonight to discuss all with you. Please inform Madam Walcote of that.'

He gave his leave to Christopher and Nigellus and left quickly. Nigellus was left in the company of Christopher.

'You know something,' said Nigellus, studying the boy. 'You remind me of someone.' The boy ducked his head as Nigellus gathered his gown around him and stepped after John and Madam Walcote. 'Oh, well. I'm sure I'll think of whom anon.'

FIFTEEN

Crispin alerted the steward about the candlestick and told him not to expect the stonemason's return. 'Who was it that hired all the workmen, Master Able? Was it you?'

'Yes, Master Guest. I enquired of the guilds and was given a list of men. They all came recommended. This is terrible.'

'Didn't you personally scrutinize these men properly?'

'I thought I had, Master Guest.' He rubbed his fist into his palm. 'It is very frustrating – quite beyond the pale – when people lie to you.'

'How well I know it, Master Able.'

'Yes, you must be vexed all the time, sir. What's to be done about it?'

'We do our best, Master Able, and try better next time.'

Able picked up the candlestick, measuring its weight in his hand. 'I have sworn to uphold the honor of this household.'

'Walter Perchay, one of your plasterers, had another worker steal this for him.'

The steward shook his head miserably. 'I don't know what you think of me, Master Guest.'

'That's hardly to the point. I don't suppose Perchay is here?'

'As it happens, he isn't.'

'I don't suppose he'll be back.'

'Oh, God. Oh, Holy Mother!'

'I understand your feelings on the matter, Master Able. For now, we must gird ourselves for what is to come.'

'What *is* to come?'

'A murderer who will not stop even as those he seeks may be in hiding. It is someone associated with this house. Who could it be? Have you any idea?'

'I have wracked my brain, Master Guest. But the only men who have been here longer than I have – besides the cook, of course – is the footman, Michael Loscroft and the gardener, Rafe Hemm. And neither has any past relationship to the people of this house at all.'

'Do they not? I'll look into it.'

He left the anxious steward behind to make his way to the back of the house and out to the garden. He found the gardener easily enough. He was standing, leaning on his rake, and staring at the place they found William.

'Master Hemm,' he said, startling the man. He stood next to him and looked down on the dark soil that had lately seen the murder of the innocent man. 'A damnable thing, is it not?'

'Yes,' he said quietly. His fingers moved over the rake's handle, clutching and releasing.

'You've been here a long time, have you not, Master Hemm?'

He nodded. ''Bout fifteen years, I should say.'

'Did you know the tale of Wilfrid Roke before this?'

Hemm spared him a look. Dark circles ringed his eyes. 'No. Why would I have?'

'No reason.'

'I don't mix with the other servants. No call for it.'

'It seems that it would be lonely work without mixing some time. For meals, perhaps.'

'I eat my food and get out. There's no call for talking gossip and other sin.'

Crispin looked out to the grounds. The man seemed to be working at twice the speed to get all in order. Already the dead trees and shrubs were either removed or trimmed for winter. 'Did you see anything? Hear anything of the murder?'

'Nothing I didn't tell the coroner.'

Crispin placed his hands behind his back as he strolled forward a few paces, looking back at the garden by the house. He cast a glance the other way to the gardener's cottage. 'Are you married, Hemm?'

'No.'

'Ever been married?'

'And exactly what has that to do with aught?'

'Nothing. I merely wondered. You like to keep to yourself.'

'As I hope others would, but seldom do.'

'What do you think of the Cobmartins?'

He huffed a breath, watched the cloud rise and disperse. 'They are my masters. I don't think much more of them than that.'

'There's little joy in that, Hemm.'

'My joy is my own business. Now if you don't mind, I've got my raking to do.'

'If *you* don't mind . . .' Crispin put out a hand to pause the man. 'How did you come by this job with the Cobmartins?'

He frowned at the ground and shrugged. 'Don't know. It was so long ago.'

'Surely you can recall something as important as that? Where did you work before?'

He looked up again with a filthy expression. 'You ask a lot of personal questions.'

'Murder is very personal, Master Hemm.'

'Murder. As if I'd anything to do with it. You're trying to put *my* neck in the noose because you haven't any other ideas.'

'That is not how I work, Hemm. I seek the truth, always.'

'So says many a lord. And many a man like me swings from a gibbet because no one has time for any "truth".'

'I've got the time. Is there any reason I should suspect you?'

Hemm scowled and raised the rake like a weapon, but held his pose, glaring eye to eye with Crispin before he relented and lowered the tool. 'No reason whatsoever.'

'Well then? How came you here fifteen years ago?'

'I heard tell they needed a gardener. I came hither and put in my name. I worked at other lordly houses. The mistress liked my work.'

'The elder Madam Cobmartin?'

'Aye. They took me on and that was it. They gave me yon cottage and I do my work, as per the new Madam Cobmartin's instructions.'

'It looks as if you were a bit of a slacker under Augustus Cobmartin.'

The man brandished his rake again, but soon lowered it. 'You've no call to say that.'

'Haven't I? The garden was all but dead.'

'It's the season.'

'September?'

He scowled deeper. 'Master Augustus . . . he told me to leave it. He said he didn't like the noise.'

'Noise?'

'Birds and such. He was a . . . a peculiar man. Like all them Cobmartins.'

Crispin studied him with a sneer of distaste, from the man's frowning brows to his tight fists wrapped around the rake. 'What other lordly houses did you work for? Were they in London?'

'Naw. In Watford. I had a hankering to come to London.'

'Where in Watford?'

'St Albans Abbey, if you must know. *Now* may I get to me work?'

Crispin sighed impatiently and stepped back. He watched for a few moments, the easy stroking the man did with the rake, gathering up the bloodied leaves, and lifting them with a hand on the leaves and the rake, and depositing them in his cart. When he tossed the rake atop them and lifted the handles of the cart to roll it away, Crispin took his leave of him.

He stood in the foyer, wondering where he could find the footman, when the man entered through an archway. 'Master Loscroft, is it?'

He stopped, and when he turned, he bowed. He was a lean man, possibly Crispin's age, with dark, curled hair with a spray of gray encroaching on the front. His beard was trimmed close and manicured. Crispin had seen many a footman, and their manner seemed to run the gambit between guard dog and varlet. This one reminded Crispin of a palace varlet; somewhat sub-servient but bright-eyed and no stranger to physical force.

But he also recalled the suspicious circumstances of how he had wriggled into the household. No, he hadn't forgotten that.

'May I have a word?'

'Of course, Master Guest.'

'I remember the tale you told; how you got into this household.'

'Tale, Master Guest? I shouldn't characterize it in that way.'

'And yet your employer initially turned you away.'

'But then—'

'Yes. But then his wife had an encounter and you just happened to be there. Just as you happened to befriend Wilfrid Roke.'

Loscroft paused. 'It was . . . most fortuitous.'

'Did you know the elder Cobmartin harbored his doubts about you? That he only kept you on so as not to embarrass himself?'

Loscroft reddened and threw back his shoulders. 'I don't think that's true.'

'Oh, it is. Master Cobmartin – the current one – told me as much.'

The footman frowned and stuffed his hands behind his back. 'I never contrived it. I know people have said so over the years, but I never did. And I have been a devout member of this household ever since. I've guarded this house like any good servant, and I've been pleased to work here. Both masters prior to Master Nigellus have been good to me and I have been loyal to them. I hope to serve Master Nigellus with as much loyalty as the others. You won't find a soul to complain about me.' His cheeks had gone ruddy, and his breath came hot and fast.

'Steady, Loscroft. Last time we spoke, you said you were acquainted with Wilfrid Roke.'

The change of subject seemed to startle him. Those ruddy cheeks had gone pale. 'I met him, is all. Long before the events in this household.'

'You met him in a tavern, so you said. What did he talk of with you?'

'It was more than twenty years ago—'

'But surely you recall it. Did he speak of his life? His desires? His . . . anger? Men in taverns who drink to excess are often loose with their tongues.'

'He didn't drink to excess. At least, I didn't think so. I don't think he told me those things.'

'He didn't tell you that he suspected his wife was unfaithful? That he was unhappy about it? That's why a man goes to a tavern to drink, is it not? To share his troubles? To make them smaller?'

Instead of the shock Crispin expected at such an outlandishly personal statement, Loscroft seemed to close inward. His eyes shuttered and his mouth formed into a straight line. 'I don't remember.'

'You seemed to recall it better when we talked earlier.'

'I don't remember,' he said tightly.

Crispin took a step closer, too close to be comfortable for the other man. He stiffened but refused to take a step back. Crispin held his gaze for an unnervingly long time, before waving his hand in a careless gesture. 'You may go.'

Loscroft whirled, looking as if he'd make a hasty exit, but he seemed to think better of it. Instead, he walked stiffly away in long, steady strides.

Crispin marveled. *Such a calculating man*, he mused. One who knew just how much to push, just how much to draw back. He wondered why he stayed a footman all these years. Why he hadn't advanced to steward. Perhaps he was working toward that. Crispin wouldn't be surprised.

He disappeared through an archway just as Jack barreled in. He jerked to a halt in front of Crispin.

'Jack? What's amiss?'

Catching his breath, Jack wiped his brow. 'It's a right mess is what it is, master. I went to check on the Cobmartins at Gray's Inn and they got an extortion note, of all things.'

'An extortion note? God's blood, what is going on?'

'That's what I wondered, sir. So I got them out of there. If they were receiving such messages, then their hiding place was found out. I was preparing to move them to an inn when we ran into Christopher Walcote. And he . . . well. He . . . er . . .' Jack sighed wearily. 'Master, he offered them shelter and I couldn't very well refuse.'

'What do you mean? You don't mean to say they are now at the . . . at the Walcote manor?'

'Aye, sir. I didn't know what else to do. You should meet them there tonight.'

'Dammit!' He clenched his hand and stared off to the side. 'Of all the damnable things—'

'I know, sir. But like I said . . .'

'I don't blame you, Jack. It . . . it was a good choice, all things being considered. But what of this extortion note?'

'Here.' Jack reached into his scrip and pulled out a crushed parchment. Crispin read it quickly and cursed again.

'How the hell did someone . . .' He made a disgusted sound. 'Someone in this household, no doubt. Perhaps a workman. Perhaps a *dismissed* workman. Or . . .' His thoughts strayed to the strange footman. But no. Loscroft was more calculating than that. And he'd never let himself be caught. He liked better the idea of a dismissed workman for this particular crime. 'Let us go see Harrow to discuss the matter.'

Jack paused. 'You don't think . . . you don't think it's the murderer, do you?'

'Using this as an excuse to draw them from their hiding place? But they already knew where they were.'

'Blind me, Master Crispin. What a mess this is.'

Crispin couldn't disagree. He led Jack out of the house and back toward John Harrow's house on Lime Street. But even with each hurried step, he could not help but linger on the notion of the Cobmartins at Clarence Walcote's house. Had the whole world turned upside down? Everything in his sphere was suddenly clashing together. Thank God for this distraction.

He didn't bother knocking. Even Jack looked surprised when Crispin pushed his way through the door. Harrow was there at his hearth and suddenly looked up with astonishment. Crispin waved the paper at him.

'What is the meaning of this, Harrow? Had I not let you off with a stern warning and expected better of you?'

'What?' The man backed up as Crispin kept coming and found himself against the wall. He stared at the parchment Crispin wagged in his face.

'This letter of extortion to your former employers. I should have strung you up myself.'

'Master Guest! Have mercy! I did no such thing.'

'You are lying to my face, Harrow.'

'No, no! I swear.'

Crispin grabbed the man by the shoulder and shoved him to his table. He slapped the parchment in front of him. 'You did not write this?'

The man looked it over and glanced up first at Jack then at Crispin, perplexed. 'What does this mean?'

'Sir,' Jack interjected, and in timely fashion, too, just as Crispin was hauling back his arm to slap the mason. 'Perhaps Master Harrow has his own documents with his writing?'

Crispin eased back. Well, well, he thought. The apprentice was becoming the master. 'How about it, Harrow? Have you a letter you have written? A document?'

He pointed a shaking hand. 'In yon coffer. My business accounts.'

Crispin flicked his head and Jack walked to it, lifted the unlocked lid and rummaged around. 'This?' He raised a few pages so that Harrow could see them.

'Y-yes. I wrote those.'

Jack returned to the table and laid them beside the letter. Plainly, they were not the same hand. The note was written in an unpracticed scrawl.

Crispin growled. 'Very well, Harrow. Stay out of trouble.'

'It is my fervent wish, Master Guest.'

Crispin motioned for Jack to get the letter and follow him out. 'Damn,' said Crispin. 'I could have sworn that was the man. Disgruntled at my finding out he was a thief.'

Jack read the letter again and shook his head. 'It happened too close. I mean, the Cobmartins received the note the same time you confronted him. When would he have had the time?'

Crispin thought about it and reluctantly conceded, gently rubbing the sore spot on his head.

'It has to be someone in the house,' Jack went on. 'Who else would be able to spy on the two of them, eh?'

'The footman, Jack. I had an encounter with him before you arrived. His story is strange.'

'Aye, sir. But that was so long ago. No one seems to have complained about him since.'

'Hmm.'

'And begging your pardon, Master Crispin, but Nigellus isn't the most . . . erm . . . observant man in the world.'

'No, he isn't. He could have done something or said something anywhere at home or about London.'

'You know, master,' Jack walked away from Crispin, kicking at the dirt of the lane, 'I wasn't the kindest man to Master Rykener in the beginning.'

'I remember.'

'It's just that . . . I never met the kind of man he is before. Heard of them, but never rightly met anyone. The . . . the men at the stews weren't like him. He don't like small boys.'

Crispin watched his apprentice carefully. 'I know.' It was seldom Jack brought up his childhood days in the hands of pedophiles.

'But he's loyal to the bone, he is. He helped save you. Like a true friend. And . . . well. Anyone what does so is a true friend to me. And I told him so.'

'I'm glad to hear it, Jack. John Rykener befriended me when I was first banished from court. And he was certainly not obliged to help. In fact, it was well-known how dangerous a thing it was to befriend me. But he did it anyway. I am a loyal friend to him as well, and I'll not see harm come to him or Nigellus.'

'That's what I'm trying to say, sir. The both of them. They saved your life. So . . . it can't be much of a sin, I suppose. Them doing what they do. Not that I know aught of the Church and its laws.'

'Sometimes, Jack, the Church, in all its wisdom, is lacking when it comes to compassion.'

Jack looked around as if knights of the Church would descend upon them, with swords drawn. Crispin couldn't help but smile.

'Come now, Jack. We must, I suppose, return to the Walcote manor.'

It was the last place Crispin wanted to be. Had it only been a day ago that he had sworn off going to the Walcotes? *The gods, too, are fond of a jest*, he thought without humor.

They reached Mercery and found the porter at the gate. Crispin leaned into the stone enclosure. 'You are stopping all visitors, are you not?'

'Yes, Master Guest. Even those who are accustomed to simply passing through.'

'Good.' He and Jack walked on and arrived at the front door. When they knocked, a footman answered, bowed to them, and led them to the parlor.

'What's amiss, sir?' asked Jack, face full of concern.

'Nothing,' Crispin said curtly. But he had been fidgeting. He didn't like being nervous of any situation. There was no cause for it here . . . until Philippa and Christopher entered the room.

He felt himself straighten, raise his chin, challenging them both. He noticed with some chagrin that Christopher intervened, standing between him and his mother. He felt like the biggest fool.

'Master Guest,' said Philippa with all decorum. 'Thank you for coming so timely.'

He bowed. 'Madam.'

'Our guests will be downstairs anon. They've settled in well. Both master . . . and mistress.' She gave Crispin a sharp eye, and by that he reckoned she knew the lay of the land.

'My sincere apologies for inconveniencing you, Madam Walcote . . .'

'But I invited them,' put in Christopher. 'I didn't mind at all.'

'These are dangerous circumstances, Master Walcote. You should have consulted your mother first, at the very least.'

Philippa waved her hand. 'It doesn't matter. They used your name to vouchsafe for themselves. That was all I needed.'

She strolled over to one of the high-backed chairs by the hearth and seated herself. Christopher watched her, sent a glance back at Crispin, then lowered his face.

'Nevertheless,' said Crispin, 'I shall make certain of your safety. Of all in this household.'

'I'm curious at the circumstances,' said Philippa. 'But I didn't want to pry.'

'I'm certain Master Cobmartin wouldn't have issue with telling you his tale. For here he comes now.'

Nigellus and John, dressed as 'Eleanor', entered the parlor, nodding to their hosts and to Crispin and Jack. John made his way to the other high-backed chair and sat, smiling at Philippa like old friends. Crispin swore under his breath.

'Madam Walcote,' said Nigellus with another bow. 'You are gracious indeed to house us poor refugees from danger.'

'If I may, Master Cobmartin, can you share the nature of it with me? I shall oblige you in any case if you don't wish to say . . .'

He glanced once at Crispin, and since he gave no indication what Nigellus was to do, the lawyer launched into his tale: how the dead man's remains were found, how the son was also murdered and that fear was sparked in Crispin that Nigellus could be next.

Enrapt, Philippa sat back when he'd finished. 'Then you *must* stay, Master Cobmartin, and no argument. If Master Guest thinks you should, I shall not naysay him.'

'Thank you, madam. You are most generous.'

'Not a bit of it. And you must call me Philippa. After all, we should be better friends, your family being mercers and all.'

'Then you must call me Nigellus, and this is my Eleanor.'

'Oh, Eleanor and I are already close companions.' Crispin caught the sly wink directed at him.

Christopher leaned urgently close to Crispin. 'Are you any closer to finding the culprit, Crispin?'

'No. I'm afraid I must let the situation move on apace before any of it will make sense to me. My priority is keeping your houseguests safe.'

'Mine as well,' he said, hand on his dagger hilt.

Crispin couldn't help but smile. 'Madam Walcote, I'm afraid there is another matter which I must discuss with the Cobmartins. A private matter.'

She smiled and stood. 'That's us being thrown out, Christopher.'

'What? No! I'm part of the investigation. I get to stay . . . don't I?'

'I'm afraid not,' said Crispin.

'That's not fair! I brought them here—'

Crispin stepped forward, grasped the boy's arm, and marched him from the room. When he closed the door behind him, he released his arm. 'This isn't a game, boy. It isn't something to assuage you when you get bored from your wealthy life as a merchant. These are people's lives. These are the lives of my friends. And I will not be a party to your trivializing that.'

He blinked, stuttered for a moment, before pressing his mouth together and nodding silently to Crispin.

'Now that that's understood, you may escort your mother out.' He opened the door and a much-chastened Christopher offered his hand to his mother who was waiting by the door. She glanced lingeringly at Crispin as she walked by him, but mercifully said nothing.

Crispin closed the door after him again once he'd gone back into the parlor. 'This extortion,' said Crispin, moving closer to the fire. 'Do you think it came from your household?'

Nigellus leaned against the hearth wearily. 'I suppose. Although . . . it might have come from anywhere.'

'Let us suppose for the moment it did come from your household. It is the most likely, from those who have acquaintance with you and your . . . habits. Can you think of anyone who might be disgruntled?'

'Disgruntled? No.'

'Do you recognize the writing?'

Nigellus shook his head. 'It isn't anyone whose writing I am accustomed to. That is to say, not . . . not my clerk, who was a kind and gentle lad. Dear me. I shall have to acquire another clerk, I suppose.'

'Any business acquaintance?'

He shook his head again.

John shot to his feet. 'It can't be anyone who works with Nigellus. He is very respected.'

Crispin ignored him. 'In the letter, it mentions your father. What can you make of that?'

'I haven't the least idea. Oh, Crispin. Why don't we just pay the ransom?'

'I don't advise that. They will only come back for more once their purse is empty again. Can you afford to maintain this churl the rest of your lives?'

'That's what I told him,' said John quietly.

Nigellus shrugged. 'What is the alternative? The knowledge they have is damning and will not change with time.'

'It can if I . . . if I . . . left.'

Everyone turned toward John Rykener. He wore as sorrowful a face as Crispin had ever seen, wholly unnatural for the lively personage Crispin knew him to be.

Nigellus appeared suddenly stricken. He fell back against the hearth as if it alone held him up. 'What do you mean?'

Rykener sighed. His voice, usually animated and loud – often annoyingly so – fell to something subdued and soft. 'It's all because of me. I thought I could have this life. I thought . . . the rest didn't matter somehow, that it would all

be forgotten with time. But it can't be. Not ever. And I'll ruin
your reputation if I stay. I wouldn't do that to you for the
world. I love you too much for that. I'd rather leave you than
let you suffer. It will all go away if I leave you.'

Crispin kept silent and slid his gaze toward Nigellus, who
had suddenly gone still. The man's mind seemed to be working
it out, each thought a cogwheel moving yet another thought,
until it reached his eyes, bright with moisture. He appeared to
gird himself, even as his eyes filled with tears.

'No. That is absolutely out of the question.' His voice didn't
match his usually befuddled nature. It was stiff and formal, as
he would have spoken in a court of law. He stalked toward John
and took his hand, though Rykener tried to snatch it away.
Nigellus held fast and pulled it toward him, pressing it to his
chest. 'It is absolutely out of the question. You belong to me.
You will go nowhere. Or I shall bring suit against you for
abandonment. You are mine. And I will fight for you. There
will be no more talk of this.'

John blinked back his own tears but they fell anyway on
his flattened face. 'But . . . Nigel—'

'Tut. I said no more. You are mine and I am yours. There is
no need for further discussion.' He turned to Crispin, Rykener's
hand still clutched to his chest. 'Crispin, what must we do?'

'Well. Tomorrow is Thursday. I suggest we go to the appointed
place. Jack and I, however, will get there earlier, hide ourselves
and await this person. You will leave the coin as instructed, but
Jack and I will snatch this extortionist. And we will put an end
to this plot.'

Nigellus turned toward John and his stoic expression softened.
'You see, my dear. Crispin will solve it. As he always does.'

John drew a kerchief from his pouch and loudly blew his
nose. He openly wept, and Nigellus gathered him in and laid
the taller man's head on his shoulder.

That was Crispin's cue to leave. He motioned for Jack
and the man followed him out. Once on Mercery Jack shook
his head. 'I thought I was the only one who loved me wife as
fiercely as that,' he said softly.

Crispin said nothing, alone with his own thoughts of love
and faithfulness and honor.

SIXTEEN

When he and Jack arrived back to the Shambles, a missive was waiting for him. It was from Philip Able, the Cobmartins' steward.

'What is it, Master Crispin?' asked Jack.

'It says that the coroner returned the body of William Roke to the Cobmartin household. He's to lie there before the funeral.'

'Poor soul. He's got nowhere else to go.'

'It is a sorry state of affairs. By the way, where is Master Robert?' He'd expected to see the man preparing food, but of course, they had agreed that Isabel was to remain cook at Crispin's hearth.

Jack trotted to the back of the house and peered out the window. 'He's out there playing with the children. He's . . . blind me. He's letting them ride him like a horse!'

The front door opened and Isabel entered, carrying the two-year-old on one hip, and a parcel on the other. She set her daughter down and the child toddled over to Jack, arms up. He lifted her into his embrace.

'There you are, Jack.' She gave her husband a kiss on the cheek, and cursory curtsey to Crispin. 'The two of you are very busy these days.' She set the parcel down, smoothed out her gown, and straightened her veil. 'Your head, Master Crispin. Are you well?'

'Haven't even noticed it. But I have Jack here in case I stumble.' He watched her unwrap the parcel, which turned out to be vegetables from the market stalls. 'However, this visit must be brief. We are called out again.' He lifted the missive toward Jack.

Isabel's shoulders sagged. 'Must you go? You only just got here.'

Jack switched the child to one side while he took Isabel in his other arm and kissed her temple. 'Now, now. This is the life of a tracker, my love. We are called and we must go. Have you . . . have you settled your differences with Master Robert? Should I stay a while to . . .'

'No,' she said with hands rubbing at her swollen belly. She took little Genevieve out of Jack's grasp into her own. The child's little arms wound about her mother's neck. 'It is all well. He has watched the children for me while I went out to do my shopping. It was a great relief to me.'

'He's out there now,' Jack said with a chuckle. 'Being a horse.'

'Oh my. Perhaps I'd best rescue him.' She pressed another kiss to Jack, offered a second nod to Crispin, and trotted with the child to the back door.

Crispin motioned for Jack to come along and out to the street they went again.

'To the Cobmartin house?' asked Jack.

'I'm afraid so. Someone must be there to help with arrangements.'

'Blind me. It isn't bad enough that we must discover their killers, but we must bury them too? Ah, well.' They set out again back to St Martin's Lane. 'Back and forth, to and fro, we go,' said Jack.

'It is ever thus. We find one clue only to be delivered another.'

Crispin led them through the entry of the Cobmartin household again to what seemed an empty house. But there was light coming from the parlor. They headed there and Philip Able, his wife, and the maid Jenna were solemnly laying out poor William Roke on a bier, with flowers around him and a veil over his face. Jenna was softly weeping as she straightened his shroud. A priest in a dark cassock knelt at the foot of the bier, quietly praying.

Crispin stepped forward and stood over the young man as he lay. 'I grieve with the household, Master Able,' he whispered.

Able whispered back, even as the priest droned on. 'It is such a sad thing. We will bury him near the family plot. I think he would like that. I'm certain Master Cobmartin would wish it so.'

'I will relay that message. I have no doubt he would do what he could. But . . . what of the bones of his father?'

He pointed to a coffer at the foot of the bier. 'They shall be buried together. The priest told us we must obtain a second coffin for him.'

'Master Guest,' said Jenna, sniffing into her apron. 'We're having a vigil for him tonight. And tomorrow they will be laid to rest. Please. Find who did these ghastly murders.'

'You may be rest assured, demoiselle, that I shall.'

That seemed to satisfy her, and she hurried from the room, the sounds of her weeping following after her.

Soon, Able and his wife left and only the priest, Jack, and Crispin remained. The dead face under the transparent veil lay slack and foreign to the youth he had been. His hands were placed on his chest and the pendant from his father lay there as well. Crispin stared at the body. Something about it stirred the cauldron of his thoughts, but try as he might, it would not rise to the surface. Instead, he said a quiet prayer and a vow that he would indeed find his killer. He supposed he should inform the Cobmartins that the funeral was tomorrow, but a killer was still at large and he didn't want to risk their lives. Crispin and Jack would be in attendance. That should surely satisfy.

Except tomorrow was to be a busy day, what with catching an extortionist. Well, he'd done the like before. Catch a criminal one moment, then go to a funeral in another. It could be done.

After a time, he signaled to Jack and they left the room to stand in the foyer.

'Can it truly be the same person doing these murders? And for God's sake why?'

Crispin merely shook his head.

'Can we finally get back home, sir? My bones are weary with this sadness and frustration.'

'I feel it, too, Jack.'

'Poor William. I wonder . . .' He looked back at the parlor doors. 'I wonder if he saw who killed him. If only we could see the evidence in his eyes.'

'The evidence of our eyes . . .' Just as Abbot William had said. 'You only see what the world wishes you to see,' he murmured thoughtfully.

He jerked upright, struck with the enormity of the whole

sordid mess unfolding before him, just as Abbot William said it would. All of it. Every aspect of it as if it were a tapestry, the weft and warp of it. It was terrible, horrible, if true. But he'd have to be sure. 'Jack! I have another task for you before you go home.'

'Oh? What is it, master?'

He rushed to William Roke's clerk's hole. The door wasn't locked and he pushed it open. It was cold and dim within, with only a small window for light. Crispin grabbed a piece of parchment and took one of the many ink-stained quills from a cup of them. 'I think I'd like you to go to Newgate and implore the sheriff's pages to take a message.' Crispin wrote quickly, folded it, and sealed it with the wax on hand, before he addressed the front of the missive.

Jack read the address curiously.

'Take it quickly, Jack. This could be the answer we seek.'

Jack nodded and turned on his heel. Crispin followed him to the street and watched the man disappear around the curve of the road.

If his idea were really true, then this sordid affair would be at an end at last. He almost hoped it wouldn't be, because the truth would be a terrible thing. And why? Why had William been murdered too? It only fit because . . .

He girded himself. He'd seen worse, he told himself. But God's teeth. This had to rank as one of the absolute lowest.

SEVENTEEN

Thursday. Crispin swung his legs out of bed and scrubbed at his face, shuddering with the cold. If only he could stoke the hearth from where he sat. He clasped the heavy blanket around him and hurried to the fire, grabbed the cold, *cold* iron, and shoved it into the ashes and coals. He stirred it up, topped it with sticks and fresh peat, and waited till it took a flame. The peat glowed and a small fire erupted. And small warmth it gave, but it was better than nothing.

A cursory knock sounded on the door before Jack entered with hot water. 'You're up. Good. Here's your shaving water. Shall I do the ablutions, sir?'

'No, I am well enough.' He eagerly watched as Jack poured the hot water into a basin, steam curling up around the bowl and jug. Crispin rolled up his sleeves and plunged in his hands. Sanctified warmth! He sluiced his face and grabbed the cake of soap, and lathered his hands, smoothing it over his chin and cheeks.

'There's a mixtum below,' said Jack, laying out his master's cote-hardie and brushing it down. 'We'd best hurry. I'm certain you want to get to the Standard well before Sext.'

'I do,' he muttered under the foam on his lips.

Shaved and dressed, he and Jack quickly dispatched the warm pottage Isabel had laid out for them. She sat by the fire in a fur-laden chair feeding a sleepy Genevieve at the breast.

Jack kissed her goodbye, and, donning their cloaks, he and Jack left for the misty streets of London.

The Standard was one of many cisterns throughout the city. The Thames water was much too dirty and brackish at times to drink. Cisterns did the job for the citizens, and men and women traversed to and fro almost all day to fetch water from them, those not wealthy enough to have their own rare cisterns for their houses, like the Cobmartins.

The morning shadows were long and he and Jack moved among the citizens, looking for a place to keep themselves out of sight while observing the cistern.

They found just the place in a shop of pottery. He set Jack to have the owner show him every one of his wares and explain their uses, while Crispin stood by the shuttered window and looked out.

'And this one, young sir, oh. Don't believe for one moment it isn't useful. You can cook over the fire with this one,' said the shopkeeper, as Jack pasted on an expression of interest. 'Just set it on the trivet and in no time, you'll have a fine pottage. It's the favorite of my wife. She says it has the most versatility.'

'Oh?' said Jack. 'What else can it be used for? My wife is quite fond of her iron pot.'

'Young sir, there is no wife in London who would not prefer the taste of food in this fine pot. It's solid. Feel that. Smooth inside, eh? The warmth stays within.'

Crispin let the man's lecture fall to the back of his attention, though he did spare Jack a charitable glance or two.

He'd been waiting by the window with folded arms, when the bells of the churches began ringing for Sext.

Jack suddenly excused himself from the shopkeeper and hurried to the window beside Crispin. 'And now you know everything there is to know about crockery,' said Crispin out of the side of his mouth.

'Lord bless me,' he muttered. 'I daresay I could sell the things now m'self.'

As people milled before them on the street, Crispin caught sight of Nigellus, and on his arm, John Rykener in his 'Eleanor' clothes. John still looked a bit red-eyed, as if he had been weeping again. No doubt he had tried in vain to convince Nigellus to give him up. Crispin gritted his teeth. He knew he'd fight for them to the death, if need be. He was sorry he could kill this churl – whoever it was – only once.

Nigellus, trying to be surreptitious, secreted the small pouch of coins near the muddy foundation of the cistern. His eyes darted about and he tried to walk around the wooden structure, but John tugged on his arm, urging him away. They disappeared at last down the street.

Crispin waited with the presence of Jack staring over his shoulder.

For a while, nothing happened. And he feared the knave wouldn't show. But after a time, a stealthy figure swathed in a cloak moved in, and began searching at the foundations of the large, round cistern. Finally, they found the pouch, and without opening it, made to leave.

'Now,' said Crispin to Jack.

Jack darted out the door and soon ran the miscreant down. Crispin took it at a more leisurely pace, stepping out of the potter's shop, and down the street to where Jack was sitting on the creature. His apprentice soon dragged them to their feet and yanked back the hood.

Crispin sneered. 'Susannah,' he said to John Rykener's personal maid. 'How unsurprising.'

She spit at his feet. 'You've got no right to manhandle me, Crispin Guest. Get your jackal off me!'

'Jackal?' said Jack. He smiled. 'Ooo. I think I like that. Jack the Jackal!'

She began struggling, but even as Crispin stepped forward to grab her and shake some sense into her, someone swooped in and did the grabbing for him. A fist landed in her face and she dropped to the ground. But John Rykener bent and dragged her hazily to her feet again.

'You bitch! And I offered you a job. A well-paying job! You whoring bitch.'

'No more than you, Rykener,' she said, wiping the blood from her lip with the back of her hand.

Jack grabbed for the woman and drew her away from John's fists. 'Now, now, Master . . . er . . . *Madam* Eleanor. Let us take this to a more private place.' He looked up and marched the woman back to the potter's. But as he thrust her through the door, the shopkeeper was there trying to bar his way.

'I won't have this in my shop,' he cried.

'Peace, Master Potter,' said Crispin, holding a shiny coin up for the man. The man pressed his lips together and took the coin, backing up to the corner and trying to shield his wares from harm.

Jack shoved Susannah against the wall with one hand, and with the other pressed a hand to Rykener's chest. 'John, I'll not tell you again,' he said.

'I hired her. I went to the trouble to hire *her* and give her a decent living.'

'There is no honesty amongst thieves,' said Nigellus. But when John gave him a filthy look, he stuttered. 'Or . . . or s-some such.'

'Where is our money?' John demanded.

Jack yanked her pouch from her belt, and she let loose a string of blaspheming curses the like Crispin had scarce heard before, even among soldiers. Jack tossed it over his shoulder to Rykener, who caught it and dug around for their pouch. He handed it back to Nigellus and threw the rest to the floor.

Crispin gently nudged John aside to stand before the maid. 'Susannah,' he said in a dark voice, 'do you know what happens to extortionists? Especially those who ply their crimes on their employers?'

She raised her chin, but her bloody lip began to tremble. She said nothing after swearing by every saint and all of God's limbs.

Crispin got in close. 'They get their hands hewn off by the sheriff.'

She took a deep breath. 'That isn't true. The sheriffs don't care—'

'Oh, but they do. They care especially that those who were wronged were wealthy citizens and likely to be aldermen. They care very much indeed, because you see, it is the aldermen who elect them to their high office . . . and subsequently to the highest office . . . of Lord Mayor. What do they care of *you*, a mere thief who would dishonor their own office and their household for greed?'

Now she began to panic, and Jack had to force her back into the plaster to keep her from sinking or perhaps fainting.

'I didn't mean no harm!' she wailed.

'Yes, you did,' said Crispin, drawing close to her face. 'Your employer raised you up from being a whore to a decent occupation, and this is how you repay them?'

'But they have money.'

'And they were giving you a fine wage for your work and wiping clean your reputation. You are ungrateful, and worse, dishonorable. So now. What should we do with the likes of you?'

She began to sob. Jack rolled his eyes, and adjusted his stance to keep her upright.

'Send her back to Madam Bronderer,' spat John. 'There she'll likely be made to clean the latrines. That's where you belong, you ungrateful wretch.'

Susannah wailed again.

'Jack,' said Crispin, 'see that she gets to Madam Bronderer's at Bishopsgate.'

'Aye, sir.' Getting a good grip, Jack marched her back out of the shop, but they could still hear her wailing quite a distance down the lane.

Nigellus turned to Crispin. 'You are a miracle, sir. You've done it again.'

'Threats are easy to make to the wicked. They know they deserve the punishment.'

Nigellus hugged John and suddenly noticed the potter in the corner. 'Dear me. We apologize most profusely for inconveniencing you, sir. Accept my sincerest contrition.'

'And, erm . . .' Crispin pointed to a small cooking pot. 'I shall take that one.'

A few pence poorer, Crispin was satisfied with how it turned out, and that Isabel would get a new pot for cooking.

'You say you suspected her all along?' said Nigellus as they walked back toward Mercery.

'At first I thought it might be a disgruntled worker . . . but the timespan didn't match. She was the only one who truly knew John.'

'But that's absurd,' huffed John. 'I gave her an opportunity. Why would she piss on it?'

'Some people cannot change, John. Er, Eleanor. They do not see the long road. Only the cut through the alley.'

'But she mentioned Nigellus's father.'

'Yes, that was to put us off the scent. But I reckoned she could easily get something like that from the other servants.'

'What do you suppose your Elizabeth Bronderer will do about her?' asked Nigellus. 'Is there a chance – perhaps a slim one? – that she put her up to it?'

John waved his concerns away with a gesture. 'Good God, no. Elizabeth would not have hurt Susannah's chances to better herself.'

'But she was leaving her employ. Was she perhaps jealous of the girl's good fortune and wished to have the girl ruin herself for revenge? You said she wasn't happy to lose you.'

'What tales you weave. It's the lawyer in you.'

'Yes,' he muttered. Crispin knew the man had no love for the panderer whom John had worked for. He thought Nigellus might be closer to the truth than he thought, but he decided to say nothing.

'Now I want the two of you to stay inside,' he said as they reached the Walcote estate. 'You'll be safe in there.'

'I thought for a moment the extortionist and the murderer

were one,' said Nigellus. 'It would have been a unique way to draw us out.'

'Yes,' said Crispin. 'I had worried about that . . . briefly. But then I suspected it was Susannah.'

'You'll have to get another ladies maid,' said Nigellus forlornly.

'Damn. Well, I can't go back to Elizabeth. I'll have to find someone else.'

'I'll try and think of someone who might suffice,' said Crispin. 'Perhaps . . . Madam Walcote can suggest someone.'

'Oh, Crispin! That's a marvelous idea. We've become such good friends in so short a time.'

'That's what I was afraid of,' he muttered.

Before they went inside, he informed them of the funeral and Nigellus solemnly handed him a small pouch of coins to take care of the priest and the fees. 'But I'm certain Steward Able has that in order,' said Crispin.

'I'm certain he must. But just in case.'

'I will hold it dear.'

He said his farewells and watched as they entered the manor house. His thoughts lingered on Philippa, the easy way she and Rykener could find friendship. How he wished that he could fall out of love with her and simply be a friend. But his life would not be his life unless it were complicated, he decided.

But just once, he mused, it would be nice if it didn't have to be.

He crossed himself, hoping for better, and made his way back to the Shambles to give Isabel her gift.

Crispin arrived at St Martin's Church for the funeral and it wasn't long till he was joined by Jack. 'We shall have word from the sheriff's page by day's end, Master Crispin,' he said. And then he fixed his face into solemn contemplation, as the body of William Roke – conveyed in a pine coffin – was brought to the lychgate of the church, followed by another coffin carrying the bones of Wilfrid Roke. The priest came out and offered his benediction with sprinkled holy water and prayers. An altar boy carried a censer, and its fragrant smoke wound round all the gathered mourners' heads in rings of sanctification.

The pallbearers brought the coffins to two holes dug in the soft, wet earth and with ropes provided, lowered them in, one at a time.

'And bless the soul of Wilfrid Roke,' intoned the priest, 'father to William, who untimely met his undeserved death but now to find solace in the comforting arms of our Lord Jesus Christ . . .'

Crispin watched the holy water shaken over Wilfrid's resting place and wondered if he shouldn't say something now. But . . . no. It didn't matter to God, Who knew all anyway.

More prayers, more bowed heads, the household of the Cobmartins paid their respects, though there was a murmur as to why the Cobmartins themselves did not attend.

Crispin kept an eye on Philip Able and when he saw the man pay the priest, he relaxed. Once the priest walked away and the grave diggers set their shovels into the piles of dirt to cover the remains, he met Able and his wife back at the lychgate.

'I was sad to see that my master was not here,' said the steward.

'You know why, Master Able.'

'Yes. I tried to explain it to the others. Bless me. This whole affair has been so difficult.' He looked to his wife, but she stood with bowed head too, and clutched at his arm. 'Murders, theft,' said Able. 'What next, I wonder?'

'Best not to wonder,' said Crispin, eyes scanning the retreating mourners.

'Are you any closer, Master Guest, at finding out who did this? I fear poor William's soul will never rest until the murderer is found. I know *I* shall not rest.'

'I am very close, Master Able. Do not fear it.'

'Oh! Then . . . who?'

Crispin gave a bitter semblance of a smile. 'I shall return to the manor later this evening.' He offered nothing more as he moved away from him and motioned for Jack to follow as they slowly made their way back to the Shambles.

'You know something, don't you?' said Jack. 'That's why you had the sheriff's page send that missive.'

'I think I do.'

'Care to share it? I mean, I went to all the trouble and all. And I don't like Newgate any more than you do.'

Crispin glanced back over his shoulder as the church receded into the distance. There was no one else of any consequence near enough to them to overhear their conversation. 'Certainly, Jack. I am of the opinion that the dead man in the wall . . . was *not* Wilfrid Roke.'

EIGHTEEN

Jack stopped and Crispin took two more steps before he realized it. He halted and pivoted toward his apprentice.

'And when did you discover this fine bit of news?' said Jack, fists at his hips. 'We just buried the man. And now you say it was the wrong one?'

'Not long. It was only a day ago. That pendant you removed from the body, a cross with a dark stone. I saw another like it on someone else.'

'Who then?' They began walking again.

'On the dead man's father. I believe the bones were that of Thomas Courtney.'

'What? But . . . how? I thought *he* was the murderer.'

'Thomas Courtney was dallying with Wilfrid's wife Margaret. For years, I imagine. And you will recall, not long before Wilfrid supposedly went missing, Margaret fell down the stairs and broke her neck. And by Courtney's father, I discovered that Thomas had planned to run away with someone's wife at the household where he had gained employment for the last six years.'

'You think Wilfrid killed his own wife.'

'I'm certain he did.'

'And then killed Thomas Courtney.'

'Yes.'

'And stuffed him like a trussed-up rabbit into the wall.'

'Yes.'

'And plastered it over.'

'I've been watching the workmen. I don't think it a particularly difficult thing to do.'

'If you were a plasterer.'

'Or very clever yourself.'

Jack ran his hand through his curls. 'Blind me. So Wilfrid Roke *did* run away.'

'Yes, but where?'

'But . . .' Jack rubbed his beard. 'But . . . if the murderer is Wilfrid . . . why did he kill his own son?'

Crispin rested his hand on his sword hilt. 'Thomas Courtney had been dallying for years. For *six* years. William Roke said he was five years old when his mother died. I suspect – as did Wilfrid – that William Roke was *not* his son.'

'And he waited twenty years to do something about it?'

Crispin stepped aside as a cart laden with lumber rambled down the lane. Its wheels were caked in mud, both fresh and dried. 'Perhaps he wasn't certain. But he returned to see William grow to manhood. He might have begun to look like Thomas.'

'God's blood,' Jack swore. 'That's horrible. Him, stalking poor William all that time. Then William thinking his father was redeemed . . . only to be slain by him. Or . . . Damn. Now I'm all mixed up. It *wasn't* his father what killed him. And his father *was* a criminal. All that praying for forgiveness for naught.'

'It's damnable.'

'But wait a moment.' He stopped again, and Crispin stopped with him, folding his arms over his chest. 'If he ran away, then why is someone stalking the Cobmartins from within the house?'

'Maybe they aren't.'

'Are you saying now that the murderer may *not* be in the household?'

'Maybe. Maybe not.'

Jack cocked his head and narrowed his eyes. 'You *know*, don't you? Why aren't you telling me?'

'Because if I am wrong, I do not wish to look the fool.'

'You're never wrong.'

'Ha!' He roared a laugh and started walking again. 'That's

because I kept my counsel until I was certain. You see? It works. Makes me appear cleverer than I am.'

'I see. It's a wise man who knows just when to open his mouth.'

'Just so.'

Jack nodded. 'There's more to being a tracker than just figuring it out. And more to being Crispin Guest, eh?'

'Now you have gained understanding, Jack.'

Crispin brooded. He had been lighthearted when talking with Jack, but there was still the problem of it all being true. And just who the killer was. There were no servants – save for the cook, Master Robert – who had been with the family since the time of the murder. And though Crispin had ruled him out, he'd never feel completely at ease until the true killer was unmasked.

The workmen were gone. Had he dismissed them too soon from his thoughts on the matter? And what of Philip Able? Did he know more than he was telling?

They were back at the old poulterer's on the Shambles, and Jack was catching up with the day's happenings, holding a sleeping Genevieve and listening tenderly to Isabel as she told him this and that while stirring pottage in the new pot Crispin had bought for her.

As usual, Crispin stayed out of their domestic conversations. Instead, he sat in the shadows as an outsider, listening but never participating. He decided a few years ago that this was now his place. He would provide for this family, the only one he would ever have. He would watch over them like some aging lion over his pride. It wasn't a bad existence, he told himself. It could have been much worse.

He tilted his head, gazing at Isabel, strong lioness that *she* was. Her children slowly gathered round her from all the scattered places they had come from, and though they were occupied with other distractions – a wooden horse for Little Crispin, a spindle and yarn for Helen, and a ball for Gilbert – they were still attentive to the soothing sounds of her voice, telling their father of her day and theirs.

Crispin mused that he must have spent the same sort of hours at his own mother's knee . . . but he couldn't remember it.

Jack smiled at her recitation, offered a soft comment here and there, and reached out to ruffle the heads of his charges. They looked up at him with adoring eyes.

Crispin felt the sudden pang of envy, but it was soon gone. For they gazed as adoringly at Crispin when he told them stories of his knightly deeds. Who else was he to tell? And when he told those tales, he noticed Jack at the edges in the shadows, looking just as awed as his children.

Such tales Jack had never imagined, he was sure of it. They were all true. Mostly.

The sky was darkening and the messenger still had not come. Isabel had fed the children and brought them all to bed in their chamber. By then, Robert the cook had joined the adults by the fire, and they all watched it dance and leap, and throw strange shadows upon the wall.

Isabel returned and finally flopped into her chair, rubbing her swollen belly.

'When are you due, if it isn't too impertinent a question, Madam Tucker?' Robert asked.

She smiled and reached out a hand to Jack in his chair beside her. 'Well, September is almost over, so I make it near Saint Elizabeth's day.'

'And a splendid name that would be, if a girl.'

'If it is a girl, I should name her for my aunt, who was good to me. Eleanor.'

'Not another Eleanor,' said Jack, and looked instantly sorry he'd said it.

'And why not?' she asked stiffly.

He leaned toward her with a mollifying expression. 'Come, my dear. Don't you think there are far too many Eleanors in our life right now. There's Eleanor Langton and Eleanor . . . er, Cobmartin . . . Aren't those enough?'

She frowned.

Crispin found himself speaking, though he hadn't meant to. 'My mother was Johanna. Perhaps that, if a girl.'

All eyes suddenly turned toward him, sitting in his large chair at the edge of the fire. He shrugged. 'It is only a suggestion. Please don't take it as a preference.'

'Johanna,' said Isabel, musing. 'Perhaps so. I like the name.'

It made Crispin think of Christopher, suddenly so interested in tales of his grandmother, a woman he would never know, that Crispin barely remembered. And how family seemed to weave in and out of all he did, even when he tried to escape it.

'It's always about family,' he muttered. 'Always family.'

'Eh? What's that you said, Master Crispin?' asked Jack.

A knock on the door startled them all. But Jack composed himself and went to answer it. He spoke quietly to someone, offered him a coin, then closed the door. Crispin noticed he held a missive.

He said nothing as he handed it to Crispin, but he stood above his chair, no doubt anxious to hear. He had not known why he had been asked to send the sheriff's page to that place to ask his question. Crispin wasn't certain what the reply would mean, but he didn't hesitate to open the missive, breaking the wax seal from the abbey of St Albans. He read it aloud.

'*Praise God and all His angels, I bid you greetings:*

I admit that when I received your message, I was at first confused. Why should you ask of me so obscure a question? But then I realized, belatedly, who you are, and that such an enquiry, though opaque to me, must have great significance to you and whatever truth you sought. I therefore relate the answer to you and hope that it satisfies in whatever way best pleases.

As to workmen in our employ, there have been a fair few over the last twenty years. I had my chaplain search and he could find no gardener by the name of Rafe Hemm. He searched further, as you requested, and did find one man from twenty years ago, who worked for the abbey for five years before abruptly leaving. We had no word of him, and our chaplain did not know where he had gone. That name was Wilfrid Roke. I hope this may help you in some way in your holy quest for the truth.

In all God's grace and goodness, I am sincerely in His keeping.

John de la Moote, Abbot, St Albans Abbey, Watford.'

'Blind me,' gasped Jack. 'How did you know?'

'He told me. He said he had worked for the abbey. I rather

thought he was lying. But this is corroborative in the extreme, is it not?'

'Not only is he alive but that he came back to the Cobmartin house.'

'To watch and observe. If he only suspected that his son was not of his blood, he had to know. And he festered for two decades. But it is a sore thing to kill one's own flesh and blood without proof and there was none left alive to even ask the question. And so he waited, all the long years. His son would not recognize him. And perhaps he wore that beard now but hadn't then. His son was a child of five years only when he ran away. And when he returned, the boy was ten. William would never recognize him. Wilfrid must have listened to old talk of the servant who stole a relic and ran away with a certain sense of anxiety . . . or perhaps, perversely, pleasure.'

'He must be mad. All them years, watching, waiting, listening to the others speak ill of him. It had to make him mad as a hare.'

'Perhaps it was so all along.'

'M-Master Guest,' came a strained voice from across the room. Crispin turned to Robert, wide-eyed and trembling. 'Do you mean to say that the murderer is Wilfrid Roke? That he didn't die? That those bones we just buried were not his?'

'That is my meaning, Master Robert. The family buried a workman from long ago, a Thomas Courtney.'

'Courtney!' he gasped. 'And that is why you asked of him? It was Thomas Courtney? But yes. He worked there for many years, and then he was simply gone one day. That was after Madam Roke died. There was a rumor about the two of them . . .'

'Which turned out to be true, Master Robert. I believe that William Roke was really Courtney's son.'

'By the mass,' he muttered. 'And all this . . . and murder too . . . committed under all our noses. Did the master know, do you think? The elder Master Cobmartin, about the mayhem in his own house?'

'I do not know.'

Robert shook his head, placing a hand to his heart. 'But he couldn't have known. He would have dismissed Courtney forth-with. And then the murders. Blessed Holy Mother. We all thought Roke had stolen the relic and run off. We thought it was grief over his wife's death. Though now you say he . . . he murdered her as well? Yes, I heard those rumors, too. How can one ever trust your fellow servants again?'

'With God's grace and mercy,' said a shaken Isabel. 'By trusting in Him.'

He crossed himself. 'You have the right of it, madam. But it will be difficult.' He raised his face to Crispin again. 'Are you further saying that Wilfrid Roke disguised himself as our gardener, Rafe Hemm? It might be true that his son would not know him, but what of us who did?'

Crispin settled in his chair. 'Do you recognize him as Wilfrid even now? Did he have a beard when he was a varlet?'

The stark whiteness of Robert's pinched face shone in the firelight. 'No, he did not. He was clean-shaven, like you. And when he came to work for the Cobmartins as a gardener, well. He had a familiar air about him, but his beard hid his face and he spoke little to the rest of us. We never imagined it. I can barely imagine it now.'

'Shall we go get him this evening, Master Crispin?' Jack hadn't moved from his place, standing beside his chair. He wore a grim expression.

Crispin wanted nothing more than to sit in front of the warm fire as the evening came upon them, but he knew he had the responsibility of rising and doing his sworn duty. Lives were at stake. With a muffled groan, he pushed himself up. 'Get my cloak.'

Shops had closed. The streets and buildings were painted in twilight blue, shimmering in that brief color before the sun entirely disappeared.

It was a quiet time. Peaceful. A time for sitting by one's fire and contemplating sleep. Not traipsing into the cold of the city to lay hands on a murderer and conveying him to the sheriffs.

Jack's jaw was steady as he looked straight ahead. Crispin studied him, seeing the man he had become. If it weren't for Jack's children reminding Crispin how Jack used to look, he might have lost the memory of that boy of long ago. But the boy was still there in the spark of adventure in his eye . . . as well as in his gravity.

They came to the Cobmartin house and Jack knocked on the door. The footman, Michael Loscroft, answered and immediately let him in. 'Steward Able will meet you anon in the parlor.'

'We have somewhere else to go first,' said Crispin, pushing past him. He headed for the back of the house to the garden door. Once outside again, the shadows seemed to draw over their path. Tree and vine, all laid patterns over the way before them. Crispin came to the little cottage of the gardener and knocked on the door. He waited, but there was no answer. There was smoke coming from the chimney and a small light near the window, so he knocked again.

When he received no answer a second time, he motioned for Jack to go around the back of the cottage while he tried to peer in through the window's shutter. Of what he could see, it was a small room, the only room, with a pallet bed, a glowing hearth, and little else.

He went to the door again and pulled at the latch. It opened and he stepped inside. 'Master Hemm? Are you here?' There was only a small alcove for storage, and nothing else. No platforms in the rafters to hide in. And under the bed was an easy thing to see. Jack came around to the door and came inside.

'The fire's still lit,' he said.

'Yes. It would appear to be a hasty exit.'

'Maybe he's . . .'

'Doing gardening at night?'

'Oh. I'll look around.' Jack withdrew his dagger and disappeared again.

Crispin drew his and followed him out, going in the other direction. He could be hiding among the foliage, but it wasn't a very large garden, and there were few places to truly hide.

He came around the other side and met up with Jack again. 'Perhaps he sensed I was too close to discovering him.'

'I think you may be right, sir.'

They went back into the house where they met Philip Able in the foyer. 'Master Able,' said Crispin. 'I believe the gardener has left the premises.'

'What did you want him for so late in the evening?'

'Because he is a murderer, sir. He is really Wilfrid Roke and terribly dangerous.'

NINETEEN

The steward gathered the whole house and explained what Crispin had said. There were expressions of disbelief and other arguments, but Crispin silenced them all. 'We haven't time for this. We must search for him. All of us.'

They scattered. The frightened maid, Jenna, went with Able, and the others searched the grounds both inside and out.

It soon became apparent that the man was no longer on the estate.

Once they had gathered back around Crispin in the parlor, he thanked them and told them to keep an eye skinned for him.

'Should we alert the sheriffs?' asked Jack as they made their way to the door.

'And what good would that do?' He took a last look at the manor house before he strode down the pathway to the street.

'You have the right of it. It's doubtful they'll even believe you. But where would he go, sir? Back to Watford?'

'No, he hasn't been there for fifteen years. But . . .' A dreadful thought occurred to him. 'God's blood! We must hurry!' He didn't wait for Jack and ran. He heard his apprentice's steps behind him, and thank God Jack didn't bother asking.

They came to the Walcote manor and Crispin skidded before the gatehouse. But there was no porter. 'Where's the damn porter?' he hissed.

'Here!' said Jack. He was standing behind the gatehouse among the trees.

Crispin came around and saw the man lying on the ground. 'Is he . . .'

'Dead, sir. We'd best get in the house.'

Crispin's thrumming heart filled his head. He felt numb all over, could barely breathe, but his feet still ran up the steps and through the open door. Where was the footman? He was supposed to be guarding.

'Philippa! Christopher!' Crispin took the steps two at a time, seeking them out on the upper gallery.

Christopher came out of his room and stood before his door. 'Crispin? What are you doing here?'

Crispin grabbed his arm. 'Where is your mother?'

'In her chamber.'

'Take me!'

But before they reached it, Philippa emerged herself with a puzzled expression. 'What's amiss?'

Crispin used all his strength to hold back from embracing her. 'Are you all right?'

'Of course, Crispin . . .'

'Where are your guests?'

She pointed down the corridor. Crispin didn't knock. He trotted to their chamber door and rammed it, shoving his shoulder into the wood and dislodging the lock.

He stumbled inside while Nigellus scrambled from the bed and another figure threw the blankets over himself, remaining a lump beneath the canopy.

Shocked, Nigellus held a pillow before him.

Crispin caught his breath. 'I . . . I apologize. The murderer has been discovered and now he has vanished from your estate.'

Nigellus blinked and took a step closer. 'What?'

'He's here somewhere. The porter has been slain.'

'Dear God!' cried Philippa behind him. She turned and grabbed Christopher. 'Get your sword,' he heard her say as they disappeared out of the chamber. Jack walked in, staring at the door and then at Nigellus in his chemise and stockings.

'Where's Master Rykener?' he asked.

There was movement on the bed and John's face popped out of the gathered blankets. 'I'm here. We're unhurt.' He crawled backwards out of the bedclothing and stood beside it, leaning on one of the bedposts. He pushed his messy hair off his face. 'Who is the murderer?'

Crispin swiveled toward Jack. 'You go help Philippa and Christopher. I fear they will put themselves in the middle of danger.'

'Right, sir!'

'Crispin,' said John, coming around the bed. He was wearing

his woman's chemise that came down to his ankles. 'You look so pale. Are you well?'

'I . . . I feared for this household. He's here.'

'Who is it?'

He took them both into his gaze. 'Wilfrid Roke.'

Nigellus was taken aback. 'Wilfrid? That's impossible. He's dead.'

'No, it wasn't him in the wall. It was Thomas Courtney, a workman in your father's house. You know Wilfrid now as the gardener, Rafe Hemm. Wilfrid killed Courtney because he was having an affair with his wife. And he killed William . . . because he believes he is Courtney's son.'

Nigellus threw his hands to his face. 'This is dreadful! Master Hemm?'

'And the bastard is here?' John stomped over to his discarded clothes on the floor and pulled his dagger from its sheath. 'He'll not harm a hair on anyone in this household.'

'Stay here and lock the door,' said Crispin, pulling his own dagger.

John gestured toward the entry. 'I think you've made that impossible.'

Crispin looked at the door and saw that he had broken the lock and the jam when he forced his way in. 'Oh. Perhaps take one of the other chambers.'

'I want to fight him!' said John, gesturing with his dagger.

'I don't want to have to worry over you two. Lock yourselves in!'

'Perhaps,' said Nigellus, 'we should do as he says.'

'No! This has become a little too personal. Nigellus, I think that you should lock yourself away. You'll be safe, my love.'

'But if you're going to fight, then so will I.'

Crispin swore. 'God's blood! Make a decision. I must go.'

'We'll be all right, Crispin,' said John. 'Go on. Defend the house. Get that knave.'

He nodded, swept his gaze over the two of them one more time, and rushed out of the room. He opened doors in the gallery to look inside the other rooms, saw no one, and finally rushed down the stairs to stand in the foyer. He stopped and listened.

The house was eerily quiet. Where was everyone? A full household such as this? There should be more sounds, more people.

He went to a door and pulled it open. The footman was crumpled in a corner. Crispin strode to him and felt for a pulse. Not dead, simply knocked out.

But where was Jack?

He rushed to an archway and out to the kitchens. A boy ran into him, squirming and crying out. 'Hold, boy. I am a friend.'

The boy stopped struggling long enough to look up and recognition bloomed in his eyes. 'You're Master Guest.'

'Yes. Listen to me. I want you to run to Newgate and get the sheriffs. Tell them murder is taking place at the Walcote manor.'

The boy's eyes widened. It would have been comical in any other circumstances.

'Did you hear me? Go now. Don't stop running till you reach Newgate.'

The boy went. Crispin was pleased to hear his feet pelting across the floor and out of the entry.

He raised his head and bellowed. 'Where are the servants in this household? This is Crispin Guest.'

It didn't take long for the others to poke their heads out of their places, from doorways and alcoves, looking perplexed. Crispin pointed to a man coming out of a curtained alcove. 'You there! Find me the steward. The rest of you, gather here. Stay together.'

'The steward should be nearby,' said the man. 'There he is.'

The Walcote steward was an old man. He was Clarence's steward brought from his other estate once he'd married Philippa all those years ago. James Cradel. 'Master Cradel,' said Crispin, helping him from his small room under the stairs. 'Where was everyone when mayhem was going on?'

'Mayhem? But . . .' He searched around the room with yellowed eyes. 'We were not made aware that anything was amiss.'

'You did not know a mad man had entered the house?'

'I . . . I don't understand . . .'

The fool, he thought. They were told to be on their guard, but had any of them done so? 'Gather everyone here and organize a search. You have a man down in yon alcove, and I'm afraid the porter is dead.'

'Blessed *Jesu*,' he said, crossing himself.

'I want guards at your mistress and master's chambers. Do you understand me?'

'Yes, Master Guest. It shall be done.'

Crispin watched as more servants gathered, both men and women. He ordered them to break into groups and go in search. They had grabbed fire irons and daggers and other such tools that could be used as weapons. 'Stay together,' he admonished them, and took the stairs again in search of Philippa and Christopher. The gallery wasn't well lit. It wasn't all that late, but the Walcote residence kept sober hours, he supposed. Only a few of the oil lamps were lit in their niches. But there was enough light to see something that didn't belong on the floor in the darkest corner.

'Jack!' he cried. He flew toward him and dropped to the floor, praying all the while that his apprentice wasn't dead. He didn't think his heart could take the loss. But Jack was moving even as he arrived. Moaning, he touched his head.

'Blind me,' he muttered, and Crispin was never so glad to hear that oath.

'Jack.'

'Master Crispin, he's here. That whoreson is here. He took me by surprise . . .'

'Where are they?'

'I think the solar. Leave me. I'll be fine in a moment or two.'

Crispin had to take his word. He hurried to a heavy door that lay ajar. Stealthily, he pushed it open enough to peer inside.

'Come in, Master Guest,' said the voice of Rafe Hemm. When Crispin pushed it wider, he saw Christopher cradling one of his arms, and Philippa standing before Hemm, his arm around her waist, and a dagger at her throat.

TWENTY

I t was so familiar a room. A murder had happened here some sixteen years ago. Philippa's first husband who had claimed to be Nicholas Walcote the prominent mercer, had been an imposter. He was slain by the man who thought Nicholas was his brother, by using a secret entrance. Clarence, the brother of the slayer, had married Philippa, saving her from a life of poverty and ill repute. He had recognized in her the genius behind Nicholas Walcote's success. It was fortunate he had been a kind man. A forgiving man. But also a practical man who was glad that both his brothers were out of the way of his inheritance.

There was the table where Nicholas Walcote lay dead when Crispin found him. And there the window behind it. There was a tapestry on one wall and an ambry on the other, overflowing with rolled parchments of business transactions. And though Clarence was a mercer, he left the business to Philippa as well, knowing a good thing when he saw it.

Philippa and Wilfrid stood before the table and he wondered – ever so briefly – if it would be the scene of another murder. No, he wouldn't let his mind comprehend such a thing. He couldn't allow it.

'You took your time getting here, Master Guest.'

Crispin expelled a long breath. His hand itched for his dagger, but he kept it still. 'Now, Wilfrid, just stay calm.'

'Ah, so you know who I am.' He tightened his hold on Philippa's middle and she raised her chin higher when the knife blade pressed firmer to her white throat. 'I thought you might. That's why I ran.' His accent wasn't as rough as he used when he was Rafe Hemm. His deception had been complete.

Crispin gave Philippa a reassuring eye and quickly returned his attention to Wilfrid. 'But why did you run here?'

'Because this is where the Cobmartins are hiding.' He chuckled. 'You think I didn't know? There is not much that escapes me. I heard talk here and there.'

Crispin spared a look at Christopher. 'Are you all right, boy?'

His face was contorted in anger and frustration. He must have tried to defend his mother, but Wilfrid had got the better of him, for his arm was clearly broken. He held it tight to his chest. 'Yes,' he hissed.

'I wonder, Master Roke,' said Crispin, stalling. For what, he wasn't certain. 'I wonder why you came back to the Cobmartin manor after you left the abbey in Watford. You were safe, far from home.'

'You checked on me, didn't you? The moment I said it, I knew you would. I knew I had only a matter of a day.'

'You seemed to do well there. Why return?'

Wilfrid settled his arm comfortably around Philippa's waist. Crispin wanted nothing more than to pull that arm away. He had no right to touch her so intimately.

'I . . . I needed to see the boy.'

'To see . . . who he looked like.'

Wilfrid smiled. He glanced toward Christopher. 'I see you know well my intents, Master Guest. It seems that you have a double as well. It's unmistakable. Does the bastard know he's yours?'

Christopher growled and looked to be ready to pounce. Crispin turned sharply to him and shook his head.

What was Crispin to say? It was obvious to anyone with eyes. 'It is what it is, Wilfrid.'

'So he does know. What of his father? Is he aware he's been cuckolded? How does he feel about that? That his entire legacy is a lie?'

'He doesn't know,' said Crispin, gritting his teeth at it. 'He's a good man. He doesn't need to know.'

'And yet, here you are, still carrying on with his wife under his nose when he is out of town. Someone should tell the poor man. Someone should make certain he doesn't remain the fool.'

'Who told you about Margaret and Thomas Courtney?' said Crispin hastily. Anything to shut him up.

Wilfrid smiled again, but it never reached his cold eyes. 'You are apprised of the situation. So all the rumors about you are true. Well, well.'

'You killed your wife. But you also killed your son . . . because he was *not* your son.'

Wilfrid looked off to the side, perhaps looking into the past. 'It's strange. At first, I believed he was mine. Any wife would lie.' He shook Philippa and pressed his face to her cheek. She tried to shy back but there was no place for her to go. 'Did *you* lie, little wife? But of course you did. There was your lover, and there your husband, the rich man. You had to lie. You had to bed that husband of yours every day and smile and flatter him, and all the while laugh behind his back at what a fool he is.'

'It's not true, Christopher,' she gasped.

'Of course it's true,' said Wilfrid. 'All women lie. Did you run to *him* in the night after leaving your wedded husband's bed?' He jerked his head toward Crispin.

Slowly she turned her head, and spat at her captor.

Wilfrid let the spittle lie on his cheek, let it run down his face. He sneered and grasped her tight again. 'They're all the same, aren't they, Guest? I think Margaret knew I was going to cast her down the steps. She fought, but my fist shut her mouth quick enough. And then the stairs did the rest.'

'Even a little remorse would help your soul, Wilfrid.'

He smiled again. 'Courtney had to die. There were no two ways about it. It was a pleasure killing him. I caught him stealing the relic. I'll wager you never knew that, Guest. Yes, I caught *him*. And stuffed him in that wall in the mid of night, and laughed to myself as I plastered him in. And then *I* left. It was only after I came back that I discovered what the servants had thought. That *I* had stolen the relic and run off. What did I care of that? Years later I had to return, because it ate at me. *Was* William mine? It gnawed on me like a cancer. I couldn't stand it. I had to be certain. When I left him he was five years old. He *could* have been my son. Coming back five years later, I still couldn't tell. He looked more like Margaret, you see. So I stayed. And as the years tolled on, he took on the manner and looks of that damned mason, and I knew the truth at last. But I didn't know what to do about it. Until the workmen uncovered poor Thomas Courtney. I knew the law wouldn't let it go. That it would soon all be discovered. So I had to work fast.'

Crispin shook his head. Not in pity. For the man deserved none. But at the waste. 'He would have been glad to know you again. He was relieved that his father was not a murderer. But of course, that turned out to be true after all. You killed him, without his ever knowing.'

'Well, that's not quite true, Guest,' he said brightly. 'Before I struck the blow, I told him who I was. He seemed most surprised.'

'Have you no soul? No conscience? Why not let William live without his ever knowing? None of us would have known.'

'You would have known.' His expression suddenly darkened and he frowned. 'You would have known. You're the Tracker. All of London knows you. You would have discovered it and told all and sundry. Everyone would have known that my legacy was a lie, that it was nothing. That's why I tried to stop you.'

'You attacked me in that alley.'

'And still you wouldn't die. That's why I took off my shoes to creep back into the steward's office to burn those parchments. I knew you'd notice muddy footprints. You're not the only clever one.'

'Then why try to slay the Cobmartins? They didn't even know who you were. Why not leave and be done with it?'

'Because it's never done. Not until the last one who knew me is dead. And now . . .' He gestured toward Christopher and Philippa, his eyes growing wilder. 'There are so many more.'

'I will not let you hurt her.'

'Oh ho! It is just like Courtney and Margaret. Their great love endured for years without my ever knowing it.'

'It's not like that,' hissed Philippa.

He clenched her hard, and she nearly doubled with the expelled breath, had he not held the knife at her throat.

'It's always like that,' he snarled. 'No one gives a damn for the poor husband. No one sheds a tear for him. Margaret was going to run away with that bastard Courtney. Maybe she would have taken her son too, I don't know. He should have been mine. He never was. And now the two of them can share eternity together in the dirt, rotting.'

'You're mad, Roke. Don't you see?'

'I see nothing but villainy around me.' He turned again to Christopher. 'Don't you see, boy, that your mother's a whore?'

Christopher's face collapsed and there was nothing Crispin could do to stop him when the boy launched himself toward Wilfrid.

But then it all happened at once. The same moment Christopher propelled forward, Philippa elbowed Wilfrid hard. He loosened his grip, she spun away, and the tapestry behind them unaccountably billowed upward. Jack sprang from behind it and its secret door, knife swinging toward Wilfrid.

Jack saw that Christopher was about to get in the way of his blade, and he kicked the boy full in the chest. Back he fell, while Jack twisted and landed full onto Wilfrid, his knife plunging.

Wilfrid struggled under the assault. Crispin leapt and grabbed Philippa's wrist and yanked her out of the way, before he nearly tripped getting to Christopher, who now not only favored his hurt arm, but had a hand to his chest, trying to breathe.

By the time Crispin helped him to his feet and bent him over so his lungs could fill, Jack was getting off the floor with a bloodied knife.

And that was when Clarence Walcote came through the door with the sheriffs in tow.

TWENTY-ONE

It wasn't long till Nigellus and Rykener came up behind the sheriffs, looking aghast.

Clarence was at Philippa's side in moments. 'Philippa? What . . . what . . .'

'I'm all right, Clarence,' she said, straightening her gown and her veil that had gone askew. 'See to Christopher. I daresay he'll need a physician.'

'Guest, what is this all about?' demanded Sheriff Askham.

Crispin was breathing again. That was all he knew. He had been holding it for so long, delaying Wilfrid for the rescue he had no business believing would come, that he could barely think beyond the filling of his lungs and the expelling of his breath.

Philippa was well and in the arms of her husband, but soon Clarence was comforting Christopher who was worse for wear but would recover as soon as his arm was seen to.

And then Crispin laid eyes on Jack, who had improved and was huffing, staring at Crispin with dark eyes. Crispin walked up to him and slowly enclosed him in his arms.

He'd saved them. Jack had saved Philippa and Christopher. Crispin pulled away and looked long and deep into the face of the man who had saved his loved ones. This was the first man Jack had ever killed. Crispin knew it wouldn't sink in till later once his blood cooled. But he'd make certain to be there when it did.

Finally, he looked up at the sheriff. 'A murderer has been brought to justice, Lord Sheriff.'

'I'll be the judge of that,' he sneered.

'No, *I'll* be the judge,' said Philippa, brushing aside Clarence's fawning. 'That man killed members of our household, he wounded Master Guest's apprentice Jack Tucker, *and* my son. And then he held me at knifepoint, threatening my life.'

'My dear!' cried Clarence.

'And all because he was after our houseguests.'

Clarence turned darting eyes toward the Cobmartins.

'I am aggrieved at these circumstances,' said Nigellus with a deep bow. 'Your lady was kind enough to shelter me and my wife in this dread time of trials. That man was out to kill us, and I am ashamed to say, he breeched the security of your good home to get at us.'

'You are Master Cobmartin, are you not?' said Clarence shakily.

'Indeed, sir. And my wife Eleanor.'

Clarence merely swept his eyes over John in his gown. 'But . . . I don't understand this.'

'Welcome to my world,' said the sheriff. Crispin wanted to strike him. 'Who killed that man?'

Jack stepped forward, chin raised. 'I did. He was about to do harm to Madam Walcote.'

'That's right,' she said, standing with fists clenched.

The sheriff noted the lay of the land and kept his posturing to a minimum.

'This is the deserved end to the murders that began at the

Cobmartin household,' said Crispin. 'Beginning with the skeleton in the wall. He killed that man twenty years ago. The dead man is not Wilfrid Roke, but Thomas Courtney. For there lies Wilfrid Roke.' He could tell that the sheriff was only half-listening. He interrupted Crispin's narrative by waving his hand. 'Tell it to the coroner. My work here is done. His men will take away the bodies.' His eyes swept over Crispin one last time with contempt, before he strode out of the room.

'Come, my dear. And dear Christopher,' said Clarence. 'You don't have to stay in this room. By God, I think this room is cursed.'

He marched out with his charges, pushing through the Cobmartins who still stood near the doorway.

Nigellus took one look at Crispin and hurried to the sideboard to pour wine into a goblet. He handed it to Crispin and Crispin gratefully drank. But he himself took the goblet to the sideboard and refilled it, and took it to Jack, who was wiping his blade on Wilfrid's clothes before he sheathed it. He took Jack's arm and handed him the goblet. Jack nodded his thanks and tipped it back until he emptied it.

'Sit down, Jack,' he said, directing him to the edge of the table. Jack did as he was told, staring at the floor.

John shook his head. 'I can't believe it was him. I can't believe he pursued us.'

'He was mad,' said Crispin. 'He was single-minded in his task. Only death could have stopped him.'

Nigellus wrung his hands. 'I feel responsible for the deaths here. I don't know how I can ever make it up to Master Walcote.'

'Don't worry. I think you should go home. And we will send Robert the cook back to you as soon as we can.'

'We can't just leave,' said Nigellus.

'Wait for the coroner, certainly. But I don't think the Walcotes will notice otherwise.'

Nigellus took John's hand, but John let his hand go to walk up to Jack. He took Jack's shoulders, and with a wobbly mouth, uttered, 'You should be a knight. Like your mentor. You are one of the bravest men I have ever met.'

Jack blinked up at him, and even endured John's embrace, before Nigellus drew him away.

And then they were left alone with the corpse of Wilfrid Roke.

Jack heaved a shaky sigh. 'Well. That made a sloppy end to it.'

Crispin pushed his fingers through his hair and sat next to Jack. 'It was the *only* end to it.'

'After I'd come back to me senses, I remembered about the secret door. I'd have been here sooner but they'd sealed it up in the garden. I had to tear through it with me knife.'

'It was still timely. You saved Christopher from being further hurt, and Philippa. I can't thank you enough for that.' His voice choked up at the end, so he closed his mouth.

Jack crossed himself. 'I . . . I never killed a man before.' He held up his hand, palm down. It shook. 'Look at me hand.'

'I know. It had to be done. If there was ever a man who needed killing, it was him.'

'Aye, sir. That's the truth, God help me. I shall confess it before Sunday.'

'That's a good idea.'

'So . . . he escaped to Watford after plastering Courtney in the wall and came back just because of a fool notion about his son? Was he right, sir?'

'We shall never truly know.'

'But how did he get into the steward's chamber to burn them scrolls? Only Nigellus, John, and the steward had the keys and they still possessed them.'

Crispin pushed off from the table to stand over Roke's body. He crouched down and rummaged through the pouch at his belt, withdrawing two keys. He held them up. 'One for his cottage, and the other for the steward's chamber. I'll wager anything, Jack, that the lock was never changed and he had kept his own key as varlet all these years.'

'Blind me.' Jack slumped as Crispin examined the keys once more before tossing them on the body. He returned to his perch beside Jack.

'Do you think the coroner will have me arrested?' There was worry in Jack's quiet words.

Crispin smiled. 'I don't think Madam Walcote will allow it.'

Jack offered his own weak smile. 'I think you're right.'

They sat for another long moment before Crispin rose. 'There is no need for us to guard the body. No one will disturb it.'

He patted Jack on the back and he rose as well. He led Jack out of the solar, across the gallery, and down the stairs, where the others gathered at the entry. The Walcotes were ensconced in the parlor. 'I suppose I shall have bad news to impart to the elder Master Courtney. I'm not looking forward to that.'

'What of the footman, Michael Loscroft, sir? You seemed to suspect him of some ill-doing.'

'Not of these crimes, Jack. He might have schemed long ago to get the position he now holds, and it may have been unethical, but it was not criminal. That will be left to Nigellus to judge. As far as I can tell, he is a valued servant. And a valued servant – no matter his criminal past – is worth his weight in gold.'

Jack turned to him with the ghost of a smile, and Crispin nudged him with his shoulder.

The coroner arrived in due time, asked his questions, made Jack sign a paper, and left, with the bodies on biers.

Crispin and Jack made their farewells to the Cobmartins, who were busy hugging their hosts like long-lost relatives. And just as Crispin and Jack were preparing to leave, Christopher, his splinted arm in a sling, took Crispin aside out of the parlor.

He shuffled his feet, looking down at them before he looked Crispin in the eye. 'Now I understand why you have tried to protect me.'

'Your father is not like Wilfrid Roke.'

'I know. But . . . I see now how it could easily . . . I mean . . .'

He laid a hand on Christopher's good arm. 'I'm older than you. I have seen much.'

Christopher nodded. He looked like he was still searching for the words, when Crispin rescued him. 'Go back in there, Christopher. It's not like Roke said. You mother has been chaste. I told you that, and I will not lie to you. You and I will meet up again. Don't worry. Get well.'

'Thank you. And thank your Jack for saving us.'

'Oh, he will be well-rewarded.'

Christopher offered a weary smile, and retreated back into the parlor.

He and Jack had made it almost past the gatehouse when

someone called out to them. It was Clarence Walcote this time. Crispin told Jack to go on home ahead of him.

Looking back worriedly, Jack nevertheless hurried his step. No doubt he desired the arms of his own wife and children around him about now.

Crispin waited in the dark for Clarence to catch up to him. There was a burning torch on the gatehouse but its flame was dying. The light was sparse, and he could barely see Clarence's face until he drew closer.

'Oh, I wanted to thank your Master Tucker,' said Clarence. 'But it looks like he's gone.'

'I sent him home. It was a difficult day for all of us.'

'Of course. I hope I can give you this small pouch. I would like this to go to Master Tucker in a more tactile expression of my thanks.'

'As you will, Master Walcote.' He stuffed it into his own pouch. He knew Jack would be happy to receive it. It would definitely cheer him.

He bowed to Walcote, but Clarence touched his arm. 'And . . . a small matter, Master Guest.' Clarence rubbed at his face, petted the fur at the lapels of his robe. He seemed to want to speak but couldn't quite form the words. At last, he raised his face. 'I . . . I am not a clever man, Master Guest. I am quick in some things, but not others. My wife, she is clever in ways I find confusing. And I am grateful for her.'

'She is a fine woman.'

'Yes. But . . . not being a quick man myself, I might have missed a thing or two. You know how it is. But I am no fool, Guest. I . . . I am aware that . . . that it is you who is Christopher's father and not me . . .'

Crispin froze. He didn't think his drumming heart could take another shock, but there he stood, mute.

'I'm a simple man,' Clarence went on. 'I reckoned it some time ago. It wasn't hard after seeing the two of you together, you and Christopher. I mean . . . he looks nothing like me. And very much like you.' He said the last sadly, studying Crispin as he surely studied the face of his son.

Crispin took a bracing breath. 'Master Walcote . . .'

'No, no, Master Guest,' he said, laying a gentle hand on

Crispin's arm. 'You mistake me. I am not angry. Christopher *is* my son in name and all else. And I love him dearly. Philippa told me the dreadful tale of that man that held her captive, and I felt . . . that perhaps now was the time to confess. I will not tell him I know. I will not tell Philippa. As I said, I am not a clever man, but I can count. And those months before we married said she was already with child. And . . . I know you had grown close to her in those days . . .'

'We have not sinned, Master Walcote. She is a loyal wife.'

'Oh yes, I am certain of that. Both your characters convince me of the truth of it. But I wanted that you should know. That . . . my son . . . *is* my son.'

Crispin nodded. His relief flushed through him. Christopher was safe. That was all he had wanted. It took him a moment before he could speak, and even then, it came out haltingly. 'I . . . thank you for your . . . unique generosity, Master Walcote. I shall remember you in my prayers.'

'And you in mine, Master Guest.'

There seemed little left to say. Crispin bowed low before he pivoted away and strode out to the street and back to the Shambles.

He wanted to get back to Jack, he told himself, and when he entered his lodgings at last, Isabel had seated him by the fire in his chair. 'Master Crispin,' she said kindly. 'You sit right there in your chair next to Jack, and let me bring you both warmed wine.'

'Thank you, Isabel.' He drew off his capelet and cloak – which she took and hung by the door – and he settled into his chair, glancing at his apprentice in the firelight.

Gyb, Crispin's black-and-white cat – an old soldier himself with his torn ear and old claw scars on his face – lay before the hearth, barely lifting a lid to acknowledge Crispin, but Crispin couldn't resist leaning over and giving the sleepy feline a scratch on his head.

'You don't have to worry,' Isabel added. 'When Jack told me about it, I relayed the message to Master Robert and he insisted on getting back to his master's household. I tried to delay him but he would have none of it. He extended his thanks to you for keeping him safe.'

'That's all well, then,' he said, easing his weary shoulders.

They both sat before the fire while Isabel fussed around them.

'It's not like anyone we liked died,' said Jack suddenly. 'We're acting a bit gloomy.'

'Then cheer up. Master Walcote was pleased you saved his wife and son.' He withdrew the money pouch and held it up. 'It's for you.'

'Me, sir?' He took it, staring at the little leather pouch in his palm. 'This is a first.'

'Savor it. I'm sure there will be more in the future.'

'Is that what he wanted to talk to you about?'

'Yes.' If Clarence was to keep it a secret, then Crispin would honor him and tell no one either. What mattered was that Christopher was safe.

'I'm glad it's all over. I don't mind saying this was a vexing one. But you knew the answer all along.'

'Not true, Jack. As I told you, I wasn't certain and kept it to myself until I was more certain.'

'Aye, that's right. So you'd appear more clever. I shall have to try that.'

'You're a terrible gossip. You'll never be able to do it.'

'Oi! I'm wounded, I am. You talking such about me and right to my face.'

'Am I wrong?'

A smile teased Jack's lips. 'Well . . . it isn't proper you saying such, but I suppose . . . I do like to talk about our cases, sir. You could hear a pin drop at the Boar's Tusk.'

Crispin laid his head back. He could finally feel content, finally let his unease go in their camaraderie and in the warmth of their shared hearth. In its safety. 'And you tell them so well. I've heard you once or twice.'

'At the Tusk, sir? You hiding in the shadows? Tut, tut, Master Crispin.'

'Oh, yes. Some of it was even the truth.'

Jack leaned toward him. 'It's a fact that you must embellish or no one will believe the truth. I think a bard told me that once.'

'I think *he* was embellishing the truth.'

He would have said more, but there was a knock at the door.

They both turned. Isabel hesitated, but Crispin held a hand up to her. It was late, he would go to the door.

He rose to answer it, throwing back the bolt, and opening it only slightly.

It was someone in livery, though the arms on his sleeve could not be seen in the shadows. 'I am looking for Crispin Guest,' said the man. He held the reins of his horse.

'You have found him.'

'Then this is for you.' He handed Crispin a folded parchment with a wax seal and turned on his heel to get back to his mount.

Crispin closed the door and took the missive to the light of the hearth.

'What's that, then?' asked Jack.

'I don't know.' The wax seal had no signet impressed into it. But he thought he recognized the hand that wrote his name on the outside. He snapped the wax and unfolded the parchment.

All it said was:

Meet me at Bishopsgate at midnight. Come alone.
Hereford

'Well?' said Jack.

Crispin lowered the parchment. 'It's from Lord Henry.'

Jack sat up. 'What's amiss, sir?'

'I don't know. He would have me meet him at Bishopsgate tonight.'

'I'll be with you, sir.' Jack made to rise but Crispin waved him back down.

'He told me to come alone.'

'But that don't mean *alone* alone. Does it?'

'I fear . . .' He looked at the sparse message again. 'It does.'

TWENTY-TWO

Crispin saddled Tobias. A man on a horse in the streets of London after curfew was unlikely to be harried by the Watch, and so he sat and moved with the horse as it slowly clopped over the cobblestones and mud down lane after lane. There was no moon, and the only illumination besides the cascade of stars above, were the strands of light ringing each window shutter. He rode silently toward West Cheap to where it changed to Mercery and thence to Poultry and as it turned northward to Threadneedle and finally to Bishopsgate. Under the light from an upper window to his right that shed a little glow near the arch of the gate, he saw the shadow of a man standing by his horse . . . and another a little farther away.

Crispin had to come alone, but not Henry?

He dismounted several yards away and walked the horse forward. Finally, the sparse light revealed Henry's face.

He was the Duke of Lancaster's eldest son and heir. He'd been under Crispin's tutelage and governance in Lancaster's household. Like Jack, he'd raised him till he was ten years old. That was when Crispin was arrested and banished for treason. He'd had to leave him, never getting the chance to say goodbye. He remembered that face, that ten-year-old boy, full of cheer and vigor. It seemed to be missing from that visage now. He was pale, and his expression stark. Henry had grown, had experienced. And now he was about the same age Crispin had been when he was banished from court life.

'My lord,' he said quietly.

'No, Crispin. For God's sake, call me Henry.'

Crispin presented a smile he did not feel. 'Henry.'

Hereford sighed. 'You don't know how good it is to hear your voice, to see you. Ah, Crispin. If only I had time . . .'

'What is amiss, Henry?' He glanced to the other shadowy man holding the horses. 'Why did you call me out in the mid of night?'

For a moment, the man seemed overcome, unable to speak. He ran a hand along his bearded chin, seeming to control himself. But even as he raised his blank face again, there was something in his eyes, something that haunted him, made them blank with an inner pain.

'Richard has banished me.'

Crispin paused. He had heard the words, yes, but he could not fathom them.

'He . . . why?'

Now the old Henry was back. His brows drew down, his teeth shone in the dim light in a grimace. 'It was because of Norfolk.'

Crispin had tried to keep apprised of court doings, mostly through Lancaster when he cared to speak to Crispin, but the news had been sparse of late. He was not an intimate any longer with those who knew. And minstrels couldn't always be trusted with their tidings. He had not heard anything amiss about Thomas Mowbray, the Duke of Norfolk. All Crispin knew was that he was one of the lords aligned with Henry who had marched on Richard ten years ago to demand he put aside his favorites and rule as a king should. But he had also heard that Norfolk might have been one of the lords responsible for murdering his fellow counsellor lord, the Duke of Gloucester, Richard's uncle. And at King Richard's behest at that. At least, so it was said.

Crispin asked nothing. He waited for Henry to speak.

Henry raised his face again to look up at the shops and houses. His eyes roved over them like someone trying to memorize their contours and spires. 'Norfolk told me he feared for our lives. He reported to me that Richard sought vengeance for our heroic routing of Robert de Vere at Radcot Bridge. I remarked that Richard had long ago pardoned us for that offense. But Norfolk wailed and moaned that Richard had never truly forgiven us for exiling one of his dear favorites and planned to mete out the same treatment to the two of us. He wove more tales, that there was a plot to kill me and my father at Windsor, and that the king's intimates – Exeter, Surrey, Scrope, and Salisbury – were in on the plot. It was mad, Crispin. He was clearly out of his head and spewing vile lies. I told Father of it and he's the one who told me to tell the king. I had no choice but to present it to Richard . . . as treason.'

'And you declared it at court?'

'I challenged him to battle as a disloyal traitor to the realm, false toward his majesty, to the crown, and to the nobles and all the people. And when Richard asked Mowbray to answer the charge, Mowbray accused *me* of being a traitor and a disloyal subject. I replied that I had every reason to believe he had embezzled several thousand pounds from his appointment as Captain of Calais and that he murdered Richard's uncle.'

He began to pace, striking his leg with his gauntlet to punctuate each step.

'Richard agreed that we should fight a duel of honor. He arranged the place in Coventry at Gosforth Field and it was to be last sennight. The greatest of nobles were assembled – even the new Archbishop of Canterbury was there. All were in their finery to watch one of us die. But I began to doubt that Richard wished for me to live. After all, wasn't Norfolk his toady? Wasn't he the one willing to dishonor himself with murder?'

'I can't understand it.'

'Then understand this. Richard found a way to win the day. To get rid of his loose-lipped toady and his rival – me – all in one breath. Norfolk and I had mounted our horses. I had only just lowered my visor and been handed my lance . . . when of a sudden, Richard called a halt to it. We waited nearly two hours to discover what he plotted. Richard didn't even have the temerity to pronounce his sentence himself. He had one of his knights do the deed. He decreed that Norfolk was to be exiled for life for his embezzlements *and* for his character for all I know. He had to choose to dwell in Prussia or Bohemia or Hungary or the godforsaken lands of the Saracens. But he was not allowed to return on pain of death. And as for me . . . God's body, Crispin! He banished *me*.'

Crispin gasped. 'But . . . you were to duel. It was to be settled.'

'I know.' He slapped his gauntlet against his thigh again and glared up into the heavens that seemed to have abandoned him. 'I was banished for ten years on pain of beheading.'

'Did . . . did you go to your father? Have him plead your cause?'

'I went to my father. He had my banishment reduced to *six* years. But he thought it best that I comply. That I bring no more dishonor to our house.'

'Dishonor?'

'When we marched on Richard. You might remember that His Grace my father had not approved of that. And the circumstances of Gloucester's death. You may not know this, but I was implicated in it too.'

'Henry!'

'I didn't do it, Crispin! I never would have . . . I might have spoken about his imprisonment, but I did not conspire to have him murdered. But none of it matters. I must leave England. For . . . for a while.'

Crispin's heart stuttered hard in his chest. What was happening? It was bad enough that Crispin had been banished, but thank God it hadn't been from England. That he had been allowed to stay in London was only by the good graces of Lancaster's pleading with Richard. And, he supposed, by Richard himself, who in the end, had loved Crispin and had not wanted to see him die. At least that's what Richard himself had told him some years ago.

'Henry . . .'

Hereford suddenly took hold of Crispin's arms, squeezing painfully. 'Crispin, I want you to watch over my father. I feel there is much treachery afoot. And he isn't in the best of health.'

'He is ill?'

'Yes. But I fear the most that I won't be here to protect him.'

'He's protected himself for years.'

'But he's older now. His friends are dead or gone. I fear he is vulnerable to Richard's wrath.'

'Are you truly leaving?'

'I must. My father has declared it. I fear . . . I fear I will not see him alive again.'

'Holy Mother of God.'

'Promise me, Crispin. Swear to me you will watch over him, protect him.'

He looked Henry in the eye and held that gaze. 'On my oath, on my soul, Henry, I will protect the house of Lancaster.'

Henry hung his head. He nodded to the ground. 'Good. Good. I knew I could trust you. I knew you'd be loyal to the end.'

'I will. You are my family, Henry.' His voice cracked. All in the span of a few hours, Crispin had nearly lost his love, his son, and his apprentice who was like a son to him. He had thought the Almighty had spared all he loved. But now Henry was in peril. 'What will you do? Where will you go?'

'France, I suppose. Father wants me to go to Paris and endear myself to King Charles and his princes.'

'To France? Jesus.'

'I'm taking a small cadre of men with me.'

Crispin licked his suddenly dry lips. 'It won't be forever. Only six years. You and Richard were friends as children. Remind him of that.'

'I fear that time has long passed.'

'My lord . . .' said the man in the shadows.

'Yes, yes. He's telling me I have already spent too much time here. I have much to do before I leave. I don't believe Richard understands how popular I am. Or perhaps he does, and this is why he would send me away so that the people forget. But they don't forget, do they, Crispin? They remember. And I will make certain they remember.'

'Don't do anything foolish, Henry.'

He drew back and looked Crispin up and down. 'You sound like an old man.'

'I am nearing the age when I must put aside my arms. I am certainly feeling it in my bones these days. I was banished too, you will recall.'

'In loyalty to the house of Lancaster.' Henry offered a gladdened face. 'You will see to my father?'

'You know I will. And Jack after me if I should be struck down.'

'You and your Jack Tucker. I'm surprised he isn't with you.'

'I'd be surprised if he weren't somewhere in the shadows now.'

Henry stood for a long time, merely looking at Crispin. 'I . . . I hope to see you again, old friend. God keep you, Master Guest.'

'And you, Henry. Pray often.'

'I shall. Farewell.'

He dipped back into the shadows, mounted his horse, and he and his man slipped through the gates held open for him by the passing of coins.

TWENTY-THREE

Crispin returned to his house in darkness. The hearth had burned down to reddened coals with ash raked over them. It was quiet. The rafters creaked as he lifted away his capelet hood and unbuttoned cloak, and hung them by the door.

A figure rose from one of the chairs before the hearth and merely stood.

'You're still awake.'

'Of course, sir.'

Crispin hesitated before he relented with a sigh and moved to the fire, sitting in his chair. Jack knelt and fed it more fuel. It flamed brightly, illuminating their solemn faces for a moment.

'I suppose you'd best know. Henry is being banished by the king.'

'Lord Henry? What for?'

'Because Richard wants him out of the way.'

'That sarding—'

'Speak no treason at my hearth, Jack. There's already enough of it here.'

'But, sir!'

He shivered and edged closer to the fire. It could not seem to permeate the coldness in his bones. 'I fear this, Jack. I fear what will now happen. Richard seems to have lost his mind. He's moving against his own family. I cannot see good coming of it. And now Henry tells me that Lancaster is ill.'

'Oh, master. I know he is like a father to you.'

'Henry charged me with keeping him safe. But if Richard moves against him, what good can *I* do?'

'Your best, sir. That's what you've always taught me. Do your best, as best you can. It's all any man or our Lord *could* ask.'

'You're right, of course. I shall do my best. For all the good it will do.'

'The Lord watches over us, you and me. And only the Lord knows why.'

'Only He knows.'

'I think . . .' said Jack, pondering. 'I think it's why he puts all them relics in your path.'

'Jack,' he began, admonishing.

'No, sir. I know you don't believe in them, in their power, but I've seen them too. And they *do* have power. They've led you to higher and higher places. They've led you to do the good and justice you've done. They've made you the man you are.'

'The man I am. Called a traitor by my king, and living on the Shambles. I don't know that I can be particularly proud of the man I am.'

'Master Crispin—'

He held up his hand. 'You didn't let me finish. If I am to be proud of my life, then I am proud of your being in it; for bringing love and the laughter of children into my home. For being the loyal man you have been. I am most proud of *you*, Jack. And I thank God for it.'

'Ah, sir.' He could well see the redness blooming on his apprentice's cheek.

'You've kept your vigil long enough. Get you to your chamber and to your wife. I'm sure she's been awake and worried for you too.'

Jack rose slowly and stretched. 'Aye. I'd best go. She'll have words for me if I stay here much longer.'

'That is a lie. I know she is as loyal as you are. And would wish you to keep watch for your pitiful master.'

He nodded and couldn't quite stifle a yawn. 'Good night, sir. God keep you.'

'And you, Jack.'

He watched his apprentice climb the steps, dragging his feet up each riser. He thought of following him to his own bed, but maybe he'd stay by the fire just a little longer. A little longer to think and to plan.

AFTERWORD

M any thanks go out to Anne Sidell for helping me with the Latin.

And now, John Rykener. He's wonderful as both a fictionalized character and as the real person he was. Can we consider Rykener a transgender person? Or is it only with our modern perception that he is so? In a time period where such vocabulary for issues of gender could not exist, it is impossible to say. He could no more imagine a world where transgender or gay people were accepted than a trip to the moon. I hope I have done him justice in his life. He had a lot of chutzpah, I'll give him that.

The relic played no role in this venture. Indeed, there may or may not be a relic of St Elmo's hair. But there were other more pressing events going on that the relic had to sit on the sidelines as they sometimes did in past Crispin adventures.

And speaking of Crispin's adventures, they are almost over. It's hard to believe. I've been living with this character since I wrote *Cup of Blood* way back in 2003, trying to get this medieval hardboiled detective just right. Actually, it took three years prior to that to form in my mind who Crispin Guest should be. Unfortunately, though *Cup of Blood* was not to be published until I self-published it in 2015 as a prequel between publishers, St Martin's did pick up the series in 2007 beginning with *Veil of Lies*. Crispin has had two publishers . . . well, three if you count my own imprint of 'Old London Press'; first with St Martin's Minotaur and then with Severn House. I am grateful for both publishers for having enough faith in my medieval detective to give him space on their bookshelves.

Crispin was the founder of the feast, my first published novel, with his numerous award nominations. Getting into this medieval man's mindset has been the joy of my writing life.

But all good things must come to an end. The next book is indeed the last Crispin Guest adventure, *The Deadliest Sin*, where Crispin finds himself investigating a murder at the St Frideswide priory, where nuns are dying in the manner of the Seven Deadly Sins. But with the throne of England in an uproar in that fateful year of 1399, he soon finds himself fighting for his very existence as he must choose once again whether to do battle *for* King Richard or with his enemies.

If you liked this book, please review it. And do take a look at my website JeriWesterson.com for my other genres and standalones. Thank you for reading.